Pg 5   Pesant Blood

Pg 91   Faith

By the Same Author

INSURRECTION

INSURRECTION

by Liam O'Flaherty

Little, Brown and Company · Boston
1951

FIRST EDITION

Published April 1951

129483

To Kitty

INSURRECTION

1

IT WAS NOON on Easter Monday 1916 in the city of Dublin. O'Connell Street was crowded with people on holiday. They marched back and forth on either side of the great thoroughfare, from the Parnell Monument at the northern end to the bridge that spans the Liffey on the south. Huge tramcars rumbled slowly through the center, swaying like hobbyhorses along their steel tracks, their connecting rods hissing against the electric power lines overhead. They brought still more people from the suburbs and dropped them at the Nelson Pillar, the lofty tower that stands exactly at the middle of the street, rising high above the whole city as a symbol of conquest.

As each fresh batch of people dismounted from the trams, there was a strident tumult about the square stone pedestal of the Pillar. Bedraggled women, in long white pinafores and black shawls, offered the newcomers fruit and flowers from their wooden barrows. Barefooted boys ran to and fro, like collie dogs going through a flock of sheep, yelling the names of newspapers they carried. Crippled old beggars, who crouched against the iron railings, mumbled unintelligible words as they held out distorted hands in appeal. Then tall policemen in spiked helmets urged the crowd to get in movement. Some of the newcomers formed groups and joined the marchers on parade. Others passed singly to either side of the street, to stand on the pavements against the walls of shops and gape like peasants on fair day in a country town.

There was hardly any other traffic. The cab ranks were almost empty. Only miserable old horses stood there, harnessed to battered cabs that could not possibly make the journey to the great race meeting at Fairyhouse. About an hour ago, the last jaunting car had set off in that direction at a mad gallop, with the jarvey lashing the gray mare's lean rump and the already tipsy passengers singing raucously as they rolled with the wild sidelong movement of the vehicle.

It was the twenty-fourth of April and spring was in the air. The sun shone brightly and the little steel-gray clouds seemed to dance with joy as they strolled across the dark blue sky. Sea gulls were soaring and diving high above the roofs of the houses, their harsh cries arousing thoughts of faraway cliffs and thundering seas. The sound of accordion music and of song came from the side streets.

Bartly Madden was untouched by this Easter spirit of rejoicing, as he stood among a group of men under the portico of the General Post Office, a few yards south of the Nelson Pillar, on the western side of the street. He was in the depths of gloom. He had arrived from Liverpool on the previous Saturday, carrying one hundred and fifty pounds in a money belt next to his skin. He had earned that sum during eighteen months of hard work in an English war factory. He was taking it home to Connemara where he intended to marry the daughter of a man that owned a little farm. Then he got drunk in a slum tavern while waiting for his train. When he came to his senses

4

that morning in a miserable bedroom near the Amiens Street station, his money belt was gone. Not a single penny remained in his pockets. Even his rosary beads and the scapular that he wore about his neck had been taken.

Now he did not know what to do. He would be cursed by his relatives and scorned by the whole parish if he went home with empty pockets. If he returned to the factory, in order to earn more money, he would be conscripted at once. It was to escape that fate he suddenly left England. Here in Ireland there was no conscription, but it was almost impossible to find any work. Employers were deliberately discharging their men, so that hunger might drive the poor wretches into the army, which was desperately in need of recruits for the coming offensive in France. In a word, his position was desperate.

He certainly looked the type of man that is ideally fitted by nature to be a soldier. He was twenty-four years old, over six feet in height, lean and finely muscled, with strong jaws and clear blue eyes set wide apart in a bony tanned face. While he tramped the streets that morning, recruiting sergeants with ribbons in their caps had been attracted by his splendid physique, his wrinkled clothes and his tragic expression. The cunning of their trade told them exactly what had happened to him. They knew that a man in his predicament would offer least resistance to their suggestions. So they importuned him with honeyed words. He just cursed them under his breath and went somberly on his way. In spite of his desperate plight, war and the wearing of a soldier's uniform were still anathema to his peasant soul, that yearned only for a plot of ground on which to mate and breed his kind in peace.

As he stared at the ground, with his hands in the pockets

5

of his wrinkled blue serge suit, he suddenly heard a torrent of invective come from a shabby man that stood beside him under the portico.

"Those bloody rebels should be shot," said the shabby man in the harsh nasal drawl of the Dublin slum dweller. "It makes me mad to see those bowsies go route marching at a time like this, stirring up trouble while patriotic Irishmen are dying at the front. They are in German pay."

He spat into the roadway, wiped his mouth on his ragged sleeve and added in a tone of great bitterness:

"They are the scum of the bloody earth."

Madden looked in the direction towards which the shabby man had pointed and saw a large body of men come marching onto the boulevard from Lower Abbey Street, a few hundred yards to the southeast. They were about two hundred strong. Several laden carts and a motorcar, which was also heavily laden, accompanied them. A little crowd of people, mainly composed of children, hovered on the flanks of the slowly moving column.

"It's an insult to a man like me," the shabby man continued, "to see ruffians like them go about under arms and in uniforms, while the police never raise a hand to interfere. I have two sons at the front in the Dublin Fusiliers. I'm an old soldier myself. Take a look at these ribbons, towny."

He threw open his gray jacket and cupped his right hand below three rows of brightly colored ribbon strips that were attached to the left breast of his blue waistcoat. As he did so, he clicked the heels of his miserable shoes and brought his emaciated body stiffly to attention.

"Three are for valor," he cried. "I fought in five campaigns. I was at the siege of Ladysmith. I fought in the Sudan and in India. I was discharged with the rank of

6

sergeant. I never had a mark of any kind against me."

Madden glanced casually at the ribbons. Then he turned once more towards the column of marching men, who had now crossed the street and turned north by the western pavement after rounding a small statue.

"Where are they going?" he said to the shabby man.

"Just jig-acting," the shabby man replied. "Paid to make trouble. They should all be shot without trial."

A motorcar was halted outside the Metropole Hotel, which stood halfway between the head of the advancing column and the portico. It was occupied by a number of imperial army officers, who were home on furlough from the battle front in France. A group of barefooted children and shawled women surrounded the young fighting men. The children were begging for pennies. The women were trying to sell race cards and bunches of flowers. A blind old man walked past the car at the speed of a tortoise, singing in a mournful tone. A little girl in a white pinafore walked beside him. She clutched the end of his jacket with her right hand, while she held out her left in silent appeal to the officers.

As the head of the column approached the car, another officer came running out of the hotel. He carried a bottle of whiskey in his hand. His left cheek was scarred. He wore the tartan cap of a Scottish regiment. The little strips of black ribbon that hung down from the back of his cap onto the collar of his khaki tunic fluttered in the light breeze as he crossed the pavement. He halted when within a few feet of the car, whose door had been thrown open to receive him by one of his seated comrades. He stared angrily at the marchers. Then he brandished his whiskey bottle.

7

"You yellow swine!" he shouted. "If you want to play at soldiers, why don't you go out there and fight the Hun?"

"True for you, sir," said one of the shawled women in a fawning tone. "You hit the nail on the head."

"Come on, Mac," said the officer who sat at the wheel. "I have a good tip on a horse in the first race. We'll never get there in time at this rate."

The officer in the tartan cap entered the car and sat down. Then he jumped to his feet once more.

"Traitors!" he shouted at the marchers. "Yellow swine!"

He was thrown back onto his seat as the car moved forward abruptly. The people watching the scene from the pavement began to laugh. Some of them whistled in derision after the young officer, who continued to shout and to brandish his whiskey bottle as the car gathered speed.

"Up the rebels!" shouted a young man that stood in a doorway.

The marchers took no notice of the officer's insulting remarks. They stared somberly straight ahead, like religious people walking in procession behind a sacred image. They were of all ages from fifteen to sixty. Most of them wore a uniform of some sort. Except for the four leaders that walked at the head of the column, they all carried a great quantity of military equipment. The older men staggered under their loads. Their pace was almost as slow as that of a funeral and it had none of the rhythm that gives beauty to soldiers on the march.

Mary Anne Colgan trotted along the edge of the pavement, trying to attract the attention of her son, who was marching at the center of the column. She was a middle-aged woman, short and very slender. She wore a white linen smock that narrowed sharply below her knees. It

8

was so tight about her ankles that she was obliged to take extremely short steps, like a hobbled hen. A black shawl was thrown loosely about her shoulders. She carried a bundle, wrapped in a white cloth, under the edge of her shawl. A tawdry white feather rose straight up from the back of her little round black hat.

She leaned towards her son from the pavement and whispered in a furtive manner:

"Hey! Tommy, take this bundle from me. You'll need what's in it, darling. Take it like a good boy."

Her son paid no heed to her. He stared straight ahead, with the rapture of fanaticism in his intense blue eyes. Although little more than sixteen, he was close to six feet in height. His immature body was very slender like that of his mother. His dark green uniform was much too big for him. His wide-brimmed slouch hat, pinned up at one side in the Boer style, came down about his ears. He carried two rifles over his left shoulder and a sledgehammer over his right. Four ammunition bandoliers hung down along his sides. A pickax, a shovel and two large brown sacks were tied at the back of his neck, above his bulging military pack. He bent under the weight of this great load, like a sapling in a gale. Streams of perspiration flowed down his thin pale cheeks as he trudged forward slowly.

His mother suddenly darted into the roadway, clutched his arm and offered him the bundle once more.

"Take it, for the love of God," she cried urgently. "I'm telling you that you'll need what's in it."

His face turned crimson as he brushed her aside without looking at her.

"Leave me alone," he muttered.

She hopped back onto the pavement and continued to

keep pace with him, pausing at intervals to make a further whispered appeal and then advancing once more in quick short rushes. As the head of the column reached the southern end of the General Post Office, however, she stopped trying to make contact with him. Her pinched face assumed an expression of horror and she began to pray.

"Mother of God!" she whispered. "Take pity on my little one. He is all I have in the world."

The shabby man continued to rant until the head of the column came abreast of him. Then he fell silent and stared with hatred at each section of fours that marched past him.

"You dirty bowsies!" he cried suddenly through his clenched teeth. "I'd like to strangle every damn one of you!"

Madden had been staring with deep interest at the enraptured faces of the men that marched past him. Although ignorant of their purpose, he felt sympathetic towards them, sensing that their dark rapture had its origin in a tragedy similar to his own. So that he now turned and gripped the shabby man angrily by the right arm.

"Shut up," he said.

The shabby man cursed as his arm was released. He stared at Madden with savage hatred in his eyes, as he forced his way backward through the crowd towards the wall of the building.

"Another bloody traitor!" he muttered.

At that moment, one of the column leaders jumped onto the pavement and drew his revolver.

"Halt!" he cried.

The cry was so loud and sudden that Madden almost leaped into the air. Then he gaped at the procession of

10

men, who were coming to a halt without order or precision, each crowding the other, like tired schoolboys after a long walk.

"Left turn!" continued the leader.

Encumbered by their heavy loads and by the disorder in which they had halted, the men obeyed this second command even more awkwardly than the first, jostling one another as they strove to form two ranks and face the building. Even so, Madden became nervous of them. Their tragic expressions, which aroused a feeling of kinship in him through pity, had now disappeared. They looked fierce.

Just then he became aware of Mrs. Colgan, who had halted right in front of him. Her manifest terror added to his uneasiness.

"Jesus, Mary and Joseph!" he heard her mutter in a choking voice.

Then the leader pointed his revolver at the building and cried out:

"The General Post Office! Charge!"

Mrs. Colgan shrieked as the men of the column came rushing towards her. Then she gripped Madden's waist to save herself from being knocked down and trampled underfoot.

"Jesus, Mary and Joseph!" she wailed.

Madden stooped, caught the little creature in his arms and swung her round against a column of the portico, offering his own back to the charge. There he stood for about ten seconds, receiving sharp blows from the rifles and crowbars and sledgehammers and pickaxes that were carried past him awkwardly by the wildly charging men. Then he lifted her bodily and ran with her into the road-

11

way. He scarcely noticed her weight, she was so light. She trembled in his arms like a caught bird. He put her down beside a halted tramcar south of the Nelson Pillar.

"Are you all right, ma'am?" he said.

She leaned against him, panting for breath. Then she stiffened and looked towards the General Post Office.

"My Tommy is gone in there," she wailed.

"What's happening?" Madden asked her.

"It's a rising," she said. "The Irish Volunteers and the Citizen Army have risen, with Pearse and Connolly at the head of them."

The other men that had been lounging under the portico came running pell-mell out into the roadway. The insurgents had all entered the building. The laden carts and the motorcar had disappeared into Prince's Street, a short lane running by its southern flank. People were shouting to one another all along O'Connell Street, away down to the bridge and north to the Parnell Monument, spreading news of the insurrection.

"Are they going to fight the government?" Madden said nervously.

She threw back her head and began to talk at breakneck speed.

"My Tommy wouldn't listen to me," she cried, "although I did my best to stop him. I went on my two knees and begged him to stay out of it. It was no use. He has his father's drop in him. Lord have mercy on the dead, my husband was the very same sort of headstrong person. He could no more stay out of a fight than a terrier dog. When the Boer War started, he joined the army and went off to fight Paul Kruger, a total stranger that had never done him any harm. He got killed out there in South Africa, three months after my Tommy was born. Ah! Mother of God! When my little one began to work for Joe Scanlon, the contractor, I thought the struggle to raise him was as good as over and that there would be full and plenty from then on for the rest of us. Sure, I couldn't be more wrong. It was only then my trouble started in earnest. He joined the Transport Workers Union and after that you couldn't get him out of Liberty Hall with a pitchfork. There he was night after night, the poor innocent creature, listening to James Connolly and the Countess Markievicz talk about the rights of the working class and the new world to come, when the exploitation of man by man would be at an end. He had it all off by heart, 'faith, just like a parrot. Bad cess to their gab! Before you could say Jack Robinson, he had joined the Citizen Army. My little one was drilling and firing shots out of a rifle with older men that should know better than to lead a widow's only son astray. What am I saying, though? I'm a good Irishwoman in spite of my woe. I knew it was coming, but not a word passed my lips to them that could have stopped it. No, then, they couldn't get a word out of me, poor unhappy mother that I am, even if they tried fire and brimstone. God forgive me for the very thought of turning traitor to the dear land that bore me."

Madden felt terribly sorry for her.

"You had better be getting out of here," he said to her gently, as he put his arm around her thin shoulders. "If this is a rising, there will soon be skin and hair flying. Go on home before the trouble starts. This is no fit place for a decent woman like yourself."

She looked up into his face and said:

"I can't leave my Tommy. I have a bundle here for him.

13

He left the house yesterday morning without putting on his flannels. He is a delicate lad and the doctor warned him never to go without them until the month of June. I have them here for him. There is a cold bite in the nights yet, even though the days are warm."

People now came running from all directions. The whole center of the thoroughfare was rapidly getting crowded. The tramcars had all come to a stop where they found themselves. There were only the clatter of running feet and the rumble of excited voices to be heard.

"Have it your own way, good woman," Madden said. "I'm going, in any case. I have trouble enough of my own already, without getting caught in a row that doesn't concern me."

She gripped the lapels of his jacket and looked into his eyes intently, appealing to him with all her force.

"You talk like a man from my part of the country," she said, lowering her voice to an intimate whisper. "Are you from the West?"

She had a face like a bird. There did not seem to be enough skin on it to cover her cheekbones and her bunched lips. Her faded blue eyes were sunk deeply beneath her furrowed forehead. They were constantly in movement. Her scant brown hair was drawn stiffly back into a little knot at the nape of her neck.

Madden shrewdly understood the purpose of her wheedling tone.

"I'm from Connemara," he said gruffly.

"I knew it," she cried eagerly. "I knew it by your voice. Why wouldn't I, darling? I'm from Connemara myself. I was born in the Maam Valley. My maiden name was Joyce. I came to Dublin and married a man called Colgan. Mary

14

Anne Colgan is my name. Ah! God bless you, sonny, your fine honest face could come from nowhere but Connemara."

At that moment several shots were fired within the seized building. She trembled and made the sign of the cross.

"Mother of God!" she prayed. "Have pity on me!"

The crowd had now grown to an enormous size. The whole roadway was densely packed, except for a small space in front of the General Post Office. This empty space was like a semicircular courtyard, walled by human bodies, fronting the Grecian columns of the portico. People came rushing out through the doors by which the insurgents had entered. Some women among these fugitives were screaming hysterically. They crossed the open space at a run and disappeared into the crowd, from which a rolling murmur now issued like the sound of distant thunder.

The continuous clanging of tramcar bells rose stridently above the murmur of voices, as the conductors began to remove the cars that had got surrounded by the mob. Fearful of their lives, the policemen on duty deserted their posts and leaped onto the platforms with the conductors. There they removed and hid their spiked helmets, lest these symbols of alien rule might attract the vengeance of the people. Then they crouched low as the lofty vehicles bore forward inch by inch through the compact mob.

One of these policemen had boarded the car that stood directly behind Madden. He was a lean man of great size. As he squatted on his heels beside the conductor, he clutched his helmet against his chest within his crossed arms, as if it were an object of great value that he was trying to protect. His skull was long and narrow. His thinning fair hair was combed straight forward along his sweating crown, making a jagged line above his pale receding forehead. His little gray eyes stared fixedly at the platform. His lips were drawn far back from his large upper teeth in a grin of panic. The car in which he hid, being nearest to the Pillar, was the last to get in motion. When it finally edged forward, he brought his lips together, drew his left arm back from his helmet, knelt on one knee, clenched his fist and stared over his right shoulder straight into Madden's face. The look of panic in his eyes was now joined by an expression of grim determination to make good his escape.

Madden became infected by the uncouth policeman's panic. He got angry with the little woman for trying to prey on his pity.

"Let go of me," he said in a brutal tone, as he seized her hands in order to dislodge them from his jacket lapels. "I'm getting out of here, good woman."

The whole crowd surged forward at that moment, as if obeying a single will.

"Jesus, Mary and Joseph!" cried Mrs. Colgan.

She leaped onto Madden's chest and put her arms about his neck, while still clutching her bundle. Her bony knees bore into his stomach.

"Let go of me," he shouted, struggling to get rid of her.

Unable to dislodge the hysterical creature, he put his arms about her as they were borne forward by the mass. Her shawl had slipped from her shoulders. He clasped one end of it against her spine. The other end trailed along the ground. She looked like a big skinny child in her white smock, clinging to him that way, with her black hat pressed against his cheek and her tawdry white feather on a level with the peak of his gray tweed cap.

16

The crowd halted just short of the portico, like a wave that has spent its force. He put her down close to the spot where he had stood before. Then he took her by the shoulders and shook her rudely.

"Why don't you go home?" he shouted at her.

"I can't go, sonny," she moaned.

A bald-headed man came out of the General Post Office at a headlong run. His waistcoat was unbuttoned. He carried his jacket in his left hand, trailing along his leg. There were black elastic bands on the sleeves of his white shirt above the elbows. His fat face was brick red. He wore clipped gray mustaches. His eyes were half closed and the skin about them was contracted, as with a man coming suddenly from a dark room into the light of day. His portly stomach heaved with his strained breathing.

"It's an outrage," he cried, as he halted at the edge of the crowd, beside Madden and Mrs. Colgan. "I have been a civil servant for twenty-five years. Now I've been thrown into the street by a gang of hooligans."

"For the love of God, sir," said Mrs. Colgan to him in a piteous tone, "tell me was there anybody hurt in there?"

The bald-headed man looked at her arrogantly and drew himself to his full height. Then he pulled on his jacket hurriedly, put his hand into his inside breast pocket and smiled.

"I had quite forgotten that I always carry a second pair," he said, as he took a spectacle case from his pocket.

He put on the spectacles, coughed in his throat and looked out over the heads of the multitude. He again became arrogant.

"The ruffian slapped my face," he cried as he buttoned his waistcoat hurriedly, "when I expressed my views with

17

some heat. He knocked my spectacles to the floor and dragged me away brutally when I tried to recover them. They have arrested the constable that was on duty in the public room. They also seized a military officer that was there on business. The soldiers on guard upstairs could do nothing. Believe it or not, they had been given no ammunition for their rifles."

"Was there anybody hurt, sir?" Mrs. Colgan asked again.

This time the bald-headed man did not even deign to look at her.

"Mark my words," he continued, "the government will now be forced to take drastic measures. It has been far too lenient with these ruffians, letting them go about the streets in arms, staging mock battles and threatening rebellion at public meetings. Now, though, civil servants have been insulted and a public building has been . . ."

He turned round abruptly on hearing the crash of breaking glass. His mouth opened wide as he saw an insurgent smash one of the tall domed windows to the rear of the portico with a sledgehammer.

"By Jove!" he muttered timidly, as he began to force his way back through the crowd. "These fellows seem to be in earnest after all."

The whole crowd pulled back a little way and gaped in silence at the insurgents, who were smashing all the fifteen windows on the ground floor of the seized building. Fragments of the glass slithered with a musical jingle across the broad pavement and onto the roadway. All three stories were now occupied. Insurgents appeared on the roof among the twelve statues that stood there behind a balustrade.

Then the awed silence of the multitude was broken by a

group of women, who began to shout abuse at the insurgents. They were the wives of soldiers on active service. They had been ejected from the building while waiting to draw their separation allowance.

One of these women strode onto the pavement and challenged the insurgents to come out and fight her. She was a big rawboned creature of forty, with a long fair face and fierce gray eyes. Her golden hair hung down in a disorderly plait over the back of a shaggy gray overcoat that reached to her heels.

"I'm Kate Mulcahy," she cried, as she strutted back and forth between two columns of the portico, kicking savagely at the pieces of broken glass and striking her flat bosom with her clenched fists. "I challenge the best man among ye to come and have it out with me. I'm the mother of six fine children and I could make six more in spite of my age, without having to light candles in front of blessed statues like some people I could name. I have Irish courage in my belly. I'm as powerful a woman as ever walked this bloody street. There isn't a man in Dublin that I couldn't lick, barring my husband Sergeant Jack Mulcahy of the Munster Fusiliers. Come out here to me now and I'll show the world how good I am. Come on out, ye bloody gougers."

The insurgents began to fortify the building as the woman finished speaking. Tommy Colgan appeared at the window directly in front of her. He had a number of big ledgers in his arms.

"There's my Tommy," cried Mrs. Colgan excitedly as she ran forward.

The lad was putting the ledgers on the floor, one on top of the other, when he saw her approach. He blushed deeply.

19

"Where are you going?" he whispered angrily.

She stooped and offered him the little white bundle.

"Take this, darling," she said.

"Go on away and don't disgrace me," Tommy said, as he pushed aside the bundle with his elbow. "Go home out of that."

"Take it, darling," she insisted. "You might get your death of cold unless you put on these flannels."

He again thrust aside the bundle and said:

"Leave me alone."

Another insurgent came forward at that moment. He threw down some ledgers, took the bundle from Mrs. Colgan and thrust it against Tommy's chest.

"That's no way to treat your mother," he said gruffly.

The lad took the bundle and turned away. Then he glanced over his shoulder at his mother. For a moment, his love for her mastered the dark rapture that had made him take up arms. His eyes grew soft with yearning.

"Thanks, Mother," he whispered.

Then he drew back his shoulders and marched across the floor towards the interior of the building, making a loud clatter with his hobnailed boots.

"Take it easy, ma'am," the other insurgent said to Mrs. Colgan.

She crossed herself and walked slowly back across the pavement with bowed head until she reached Kate Mulcahy, who stood wide-legged and menacing across her path.

"So that's how you raised your brat," said the golden-haired woman, with her clenched fists on her hips. "The young scut! If I could lay hands on him, I'd teach him the lesson you should have taught him. I'd settle his hash."

20

Mrs. Colgan turned on her courageously.

"He needs no lesson from a person like you," she cried. "I have no reason to feel ashamed of the way I raised him. I did it alone, too, without anybody to help me, although God didn't give me much strength the day I was born. I was never beholden to anybody for the bite and sup that went into his mouth, nor for the cloth that covered him. No, then, I was never beholden to anybody but Almighty God and His Blessed Mother. I am only a poor charwoman, but I can hold my head as high as the next. I never begged, nor borrowed nor stole. I never handled a morsel that I didn't earn with my own sweat. As for my son, his parish priest will tell you what kind of a lad he is. He will, 'faith. Father John Fallon will tell you, same as he told Joe Scanlon when my Tommy was being hired, that there isn't a more God-fearing lad in the whole parish. He neither drinks nor smokes and not a wicked word ever passed his lips. Nor am I ashamed of what he is doing now, either, although it's breaking my heart. God's will be done. It's for Him to decide what is to be. He gave me my son and He has the right to take back what He gave. I bow low before His will. I'll tell you this, though, in spite of being his mother and having only him in the whole world and being in mortal fear of losing him."

She paused dramatically, drew back a little, clenched her fists and added with great force:

"I'm proud to see my Tommy shoulder a gun for old Ireland."

Kate Mulcahy hunched her shoulders and pulled back the sleeves of her shaggy overcoat from her powerful wrists.

"You dirty little snipther of a creature!" she growled.

21

"I'm going to choke the life out of you for giving lip to the wife of a full sergeant in the Munster Fusiliers."

Madden stepped forward and took Mrs. Colgan by the arm.

"That's enough now," he said. "Come on away."

"I'm not afraid of her," Mrs. Colgan cried dauntlessly, as she disengaged her arm. "I'm little, but I can hold my ground as well as the next."

Kate Mulcahy cursed and gripped Mrs. Colgan by the throat.

"I'll squeeze the bloody daylight out of you," she shouted.

Mrs. Colgan put up her little hands and clawed at the golden-haired woman's face. She looked like a cornered rabbit as she tried to defend herself, rapping at a powerful enemy with inept paws.

"Enough of that," Madden said to Kate Mulcahy.

He seized her arms, broke her grip and pushed her aside. Then he drew Mrs. Colgan out into the roadway.

"So you're her fancy man, are you?" Kate Mulcahy shouted after him, as she wiped her scratched face with the back of her hand. "Well! Take this for your trouble, my bully boy."

She plunged forward and swung her right fist to the side of his head. He warded off the blow with his raised shoulder. Then she leaped onto his back and tried to get a stranglehold about his neck with her locked arms. He opened out his shoulders and struck her in the sides with his elbows. She stumbled as she reeled back and fell flat on her rump, cursing at the top of her voice.

The other soldiers' wives raised her to her feet and then urged the mob to attack Madden with shrill cries.

22

"Aw! Did you see the bowsie strike the poor creature?" cried a gap-toothed woman who carried an empty jug within her shawl. "The dirty coward knocked a woman down and nobody barred him. Isn't there a decent man in the crowd to chastise him?"

A tall young fellow elbowed his way forward from the center of the thoroughfare in answer to this appeal. He had curly black hair and buckteeth. The backs of his hands were tattooed. He wore a blue jersey, gray trousers and a black cap, whose peak was turned to the back of his head. The sweat rag of a ship's fireman was knotted at his throat. The rims of his eyes were black with coal dust. He stood in front of Madden and spat on his hands.

"Come on and fight your match," he cried.

As Madden thrust Mrs. Colgan aside, the young man with buckteeth rushed to the attack, swinging both fists with great skill. They landed on either side of Madden's chin almost simultaneously.

"That'll teach you manners," cried the young man with buckteeth.

Madden went down under the hard blows. A woman kicked him in the side as he fell. He got to his hands and knees at once, shook himself and then charged his opponent like a bull. The man with buckteeth grunted as Madden's head struck him in the pit of the stomach. He reeled back, stooped and gasped for breath. Madden straightened himself, stepped forward and swung his right fist with all his force. The blow landed squarely on his opponent's mouth. The man with buckteeth was almost lifted from the ground. He staggered back several yards through the crowd, which had opened to make room for the fight. Then he fell in a heap. As the enraged Madden

23

leaped forward in pursuit, five other men came at him. They were nimble little fellows from the slums. Two of them seized his arms, while the other three struck at his head, dodging back and forth like terrier dogs. Again he opened out his shoulders and shook loose his arms. In a few moments he had floored three of his attackers, only to find four more leaping at him from the crowd.

"Is there nobody from the West here?" Mrs. Colgan shouted. "Is there nobody here to give a Connemara man fair play?"

She was answered by a red-haired cattle drover, who stood head and shoulders above the crowd, about twenty yards away. A heavy brown frieze overcoat, whose skirts were caked with mire, hung loose about his lanky frame. Gray woolen socks, with white tops, were drawn up over his trouser legs almost to his knees. His rosy cheeks were mottled by alcohol. The upper parts of his ears stuck out almost at right angles to his skull.

"There is, 'faith," he shouted. "There's a man from the West here and a good one."

He clamped his hat down hard on his head, gripped his ash plant with both hands and forced a passage with his elbows to the spot where Madden was now being attacked by more than a dozen men and women, who used their fists and feet and sticks and bottles in an effort to overwhelm him.

"Up Castlebar!" cried the cattle drover, as he raised his stick.

The supple ash plant almost bent double as it collided with a slum dweller's skull. The stricken man collapsed under the blow.

"Up Castlebar!" repeated the cattle drover, as he smote another man.

With three more blows, he disabled all who were attacking Madden from the rear. Then he stood back to back with the Connemara man.

"Have no fear now," he cried jovially. "There's a Mayo man with you. Up Castlebar!"

"Come on, lads," screamed the gap-toothed woman, as she waved her empty jug. "Don't let it be said that two bog-trotters from the West can lick the whole of Dublin."

Madden and the cattle drover were being overwhelmed, in spite of their valiant efforts, when another mass of people suddenly pressed southwards on either side of the Nelson Pillar. The crowd in front of the General Post Office was carried along about fifty yards by the pressure. The group of fighters was scattered, its members being forced into different directions by the rolling wave of human bodies. As if they carried the virus of disorder on their persons, a fresh struggle developed about each of the scattered individuals. When the mass again became stationary, its surface was broken at hundreds of points by raised fists and sticks, as young men struck at one another without apparent cause. The murmur of the vast multitude had now risen to an angry roar.

Madden came to a halt out in the middle of the thoroughfare. He stood still for a few moments with his arms hanging down by his sides, stunned by the savage punishment he had received. Blood streamed from his nose. There was a sharp pain in his side where the woman had kicked him. Then he remembered Mrs. Colgan and looked about him in search of her. Finding no trace of the little woman in his neighborhood, he plunged northwards

25

towards the spot where he had last seen her. He had not gone far when he collided with a large man who wore a dark blue overcoat and a bowler hat. The large man promptly struck him on the right ear and knocked him down. Oddly enough, this fresh blow had the effect of bringing him completely to his senses. He jumped to his feet in order to cope with his new opponent. The man in the bowler hat, however, had already disappeared.

A volley of rifle shots came from the General Post Office. He looked and saw that two large flags had been hoisted on poles at the two corners of the roof. The insurgents stationed up there among the statues were cheering as they waved their rifles above their heads. A few people among the crowd joined in the cheering.

Then he heard a woman who stood directly in front of him begin to speak in a tone of gentle rapture. She was very fat and so short that the top of her hat was on a level with his throat. Although more than fifty years of age, her face had the innocent expression of a little girl. Her rosy cheeks were dotted with pimples. Her blue eyes shone in ecstasy. She was dressed all in black except for a narrow fringe of white lace at the neck of her bodice. She smiled as she spoke, showing little short white teeth that were without blemish. They shone as brightly as her eyes. Her face was gentle and compassionate. She held a prayer book clasped against her bosom in her black-gloved hands.

"That's the flag of the Irish Republic to the right," she said with her teeth almost joined. "The green, white and orange tricolor. Thank God I lived to see it raised. The one on the left, the green flag with a gold harp embroidered on its center, is the one James Connolly raised over Liberty Hall a week ago last . . ."

She groaned and stepped back as a man's elbow was thrust hard against her stomach. Madden's head was thrown forward when her shoulders struck his chest. A few drops of blood from his nose fell onto her hat. Her face looked pained for a moment. Then her trembling body stiffened and she smiled again in gentle rapture.

"Thank God I lived to see this glorious day," she whispered in an exultant tone. "No matter what happens to this rising, the Irish people will never again submit to slavery. They have been redeemed by the courage of a few. They will go on and on from this day, in arms, until their tree of liberty is in full bloom."

When Madden saw his blood on the woman's hat, he put his hand to his nose. It was only then he realized that it was bleeding. He looked down at his clothes. His jacket and waistcoat were daubed with blood. That caused him even greater pain than the loss of his money. He felt it was the last straw on his load of misfortune. As he threw back his head to halt the flow, he was stricken by an access of acute remorse. He recalled how he had argued with himself for a whole fortnight, trying to decide whether he should buy that new serge suit or go home in his old clothes. Now the precious garments, that had cost several pounds of his hard-earned money, were fouled as a result of his folly. In bitter rage, he cursed Mrs. Colgan for having involved him in this stupid brawl.

While he was tortured by these thoughts, a party of men with rifles came out of the General Post Office and stood in line before the columns of the portico. They were followed by five other men, who took up position between

27

the two center columns, to the rear of the line. One of the five had a sword attached to his uniform belt and he carried a document in his right hand.

"That's Patrick Pearse," the smiling woman whispered in a tone of deep reverence. "He's going to read the Proclamation of the Irish Republic. Ah, the gorgeous poet! That's James Connolly to his right. A great writer, too, and a noble friend of the poor. Tom Clarke, the grand old Fenian, is to his left. Look at poor Joseph Mary Plunkett, another grand poet! Oh! His neck is bandaged. Ah! God help the poor man. Isn't he brave to turn out and he dying of consumption? There's Sean MacDiarmada with them as well. Hasn't he the lovely face? You'd stand in the snow barefooted to look at a face like that."

A tall man turned towards her at that moment and said:

"Shut up, or I'll close your bloody mouth with my fist. Let's hear what the man has got to say."

2

THE GREAT CROWD was now silent. All eyes
were turned towards the Grecian columns of the portico,
where Patrick Pearse stood ready to proclaim the purpose
of the insurrection. The people were now like an audience
at a theater, tensely waiting for the climax of a play's first
act. Even the windows and the roofs of the houses on
either side of the street were thronged with spectators.
Sea gulls were soaring overhead on sunlit wings. The
hoarse rattle of machine-gun fire came from beyond the
river.

"Irishmen and Irishwomen!" Patrick Pearse cried out in
a voice of great beauty. "In the name of God and of the
dead generations from which she receives her old tradition
of nationhood, Ireland, through us, summons her children to
her flag and strikes for her freedom. Having organized and
trained her manhood through her secret revolutionary
organization, the Irish Republican Brotherhood, and
through her open military organizations, the Irish Volunteers and the Irish Citizen Army . . ."

At that moment, Madden thrust his head forward and
stared in rapture at the poet's face. He trembled and his
face shone like that of the smiling woman that stood close
to him. For the first time in his life, his mind had conceived

29

an abstract idea that lit the fire of passion in his soul. Although the words that he heard were beyond his comprehension, their sound evoked the memory of all that had exalted him since childhood. Like music, they carried him away into enchantment.

He heard his mother's crooning voice and he felt the cool touch of her hand on his sick forehead, while the roar of the distant sea came through the moonlit window of his room. He heard the twitter of birds in the eaves of the village houses, as the lovely summer days faded into night. He heard the creaking of ropes through their blocks and the great rustle of unfurling canvas, as the hookers hoisted sail going down Kilkerrin Bay. He heard the larks sing in April above the smoking fields, where the shining spades were opening the black earth.

"We declare the right of the people of Ireland," Patrick Pearse continued, "to the ownership of Ireland, and to the unfettered control of Irish destinies, to be sovereign and indefeasible. The long usurpation of that right by a foreign people and government has not extinguished the right, nor can it ever be extinguished except by the destruction of the Irish people. In every generation the Irish people have asserted their right to national freedom and sovereignty: six times during the past three hundred years they have asserted it in arms. Standing on that fundamental right and again asserting it in arms in the face of the world, we hereby proclaim the Irish Republic as a Sovereign Independent State and we pledge our lives and the lives of our comrades-in-arms to the cause of its freedom, of its welfare, and of its exaltation among the nations."

Madden now recalled a flock of wild geese that he had seen fly across the starry sky one winter's night, above the bleak mountainside on which he lived. The soft whirring of their wings in the silence of the vast firmament had then rent his soul with longing for a beauty that he could not comprehend; just as he now longed for the beauty that the poet proclaimed.

The men with rifles fired a volley into the air when Patrick Pearse finished reading the document. As the group returned to the Post Office the whole garrison began to sing the battle anthem of the insurrection. Some of the crowd began to cheer. Others joined in the singing. The great majority, however, gave voice to hatred of what the poet had said: sticks and fists were again raised, like waves bursting into foam on the surface of a turbulent sea that has been calmed for a little while by the pouring of oil.

Madden stood in a trance amid the renewed tumult, staring at the door through which the poet had disappeared. The images still coursed in somber rapture through his mind. Then suddenly they vanished and he felt unbearably lonely, as if he had lost somebody very dear to him. Elbowing the people fiercely from his path, he rushed towards the General Post Office, in order to re-establish contact with the man that had given him such extraordinary pleasure.

When he was within ten yards of the portico, he was halted by a great mass of people that pressed slowly towards the south. Even though he tried with all his strength to break through this mass, he was thrown back inch by inch towards the southeast. Then he managed to halt by putting his arm round one of the standards that supported the electric power line of the tramway. There he looked northwards over the heads of the people and saw that they had been set in motion by a great number of priests, who formed a line that stretched across the whole width of the thoroughfare.

The black line of priests advanced in silence, with their arms locked, calm and inscrutable, being obeyed without question by the multitude. Their silence went before them, like a subtle element, gradually infecting layer after layer of the crowd in an advancing tide, until the vulgar turbulence was drowned by their mysterious order and there was no sound in the thoroughfare other than the dull shuffle of southward-moving feet and the singing of the insurgents within the General Post Office.

When the line reached him, Madden abandoned his hold, turned his back and marched southwards with the people. He had not gone far when he heard a heavy burst of gunfire from beyond the river. Almost at the same moment, the insurgents broke into the chorus of their song.

He listened intently to the words:

Soldiers are we whose lives are pledged to Ireland.
Some have come from a land beyond the sea,
Sworn to be free, no more our ancient sireland
Shall shelter the despot or the slave . . .

He again heard the whirring wings of the wild geese, calling him to the pursuit of a beauty that he could not comprehend. He recalled the beautiful voice of the poet and he became once more unbearably lonely. He suddenly turned and faced the black line, intending to break through it and join the singers in the General Post Office.

He did not try to force the line, however, being prevented from doing so by the face of the young priest that confronted him at his point of contact with it. The young priest was about the same age, the same height and the

32

same athletic build as himself. His clear blue eyes had the same resolute frankness in their glance. Yet the rest of his features were immature and feminine, like those of a boy that has not yet reached adolescence. They had the delicate beauty of unsullied innocence and the tranquillity that comes from the discipline of self-denial. His cheeks flushed deeply under Madden's angry stare, even while his eyes remained stern and unrelenting. It was this strange blend of innocence and strength that caused Madden to turn once more and go shuffling southwards with his head bowed.

Now he felt terribly afraid of having committed a mortal sin by listening to the poet's voice in rapture and by wanting to join the insurgents in the General Post Office. The Idea was overwhelmed by contact with the power of the Church. All his life, from earliest infancy, he had been taught by the Church to bow down before the imperial law and to eschew all doctrines and associations that preached revolt against oppression and alien rule. An urgent voice within him suggested that he should immediately make an act of contrition. Yet he did not do so, in spite of his terrible fear. He continued to listen eagerly to the triumphant singing and to the defiant rattle of the guns beyond the river, while he was driven away southwards from the contamination of revolt by the silent black-robed shepherds of the Lord.

The crowd began to thin beyond the Metropole Hotel. A good part of it had turned into the side streets. Halfway between the Metropole and the bridge, he was accosted by a hook-nosed man who was very tipsy.

"Silliest thing I ever heard, that Proclamation," cried the hook-nosed man, as he staggered forward with his hands in the pockets of a shabby ink-stained raincoat. "The cheek of these men proclaiming themselves the Provisional Government of an Irish Republic! The whole town knows that Patrick Pearse's school out at Rathfarnham was up to its ears in debt until the Germans gave him a barrel of money for this comic opera of an insurrection. In any case, the bloody fellow is an Englishman's son. What right has he to start trouble in our unfortunate country? His breed has done us enough harm already, from Cromwell down. Then there's Connolly, the socialist, a damned ne'er-do-well that has been here and there, preaching the gospel of Karl Marx. He was going to be kicked out of his job as secretary of the Transport Workers Union. That was his trouble. The Union gave him a fortnight to clear out of Liberty Hall with his Citizen Army. So he joined Pearse. Plunkett is a failure as a poet, a sick man that hasn't more than a few months to live. He wants to die a martyr. Tom Clarke, the little tobacconist of Parnell Street, is just a crazy jailbird. Then there is that cripple Sean MacDiarmada. Do you know . . . ?"

Madden turned on the man and shouted in rage:

"Take your hands out of your pockets."

The hook-nosed man looked defiantly at Madden and added with venom:

"I'll say what I please. I'm not afraid of a clodhopper like you. I'm saying that MacDiarmada is just a bloody barman. He was thrown out of his job and then he started a rebel newspaper with money that the Huns . . ."

He yelled as he was struck. After he had fallen, he held up his palms before his mouth and spat out three broken teeth. Then he yelled again, jumped to his feet and ran headlong towards the bridge, still holding the broken teeth on his palms. Blood gushed from his torn mouth.

The line of priests had halted and unlocked arms just short of the place where the hook-nosed man had fallen. As they looked behind them, however, they saw that the thoroughfare they had cleared was again crowded. Those that had drifted into the side streets, while being driven southwards, came back again into O'Connell Street after the black line had passed. At the same time, another great horde of people came pressing southwards from the slums that lay to the north and east and west of the Nelson Pillar. Indeed, the throng in Lower O'Connell Street was now thicker than ever. The priests decided, therefore, to again lock arms and turn northwards in another attempt to clear the boulevard. Madden followed them. So did the mass of people that had been driven onto the bridge and along the quays. After the black line had gone a few yards towards the north, the crowd to the rear was almost as large as that in front.

Furthermore, the priests no longer held the power to impose their silence and their will to peace on the multitude that now filled the thoroughfare. It was the rowdy mass from the northern slums that dominated. These slum dwellers infected all with whom they came in contact by their lewd gaiety, as they advanced dancing and singing ribald songs. The hungry and ragged creatures were intoxicated by anticipation of the debauch that anarchy had unexpectedly placed within their reach.

So that when the line of priests parted at the center, in order to pass a small monument, they were unable to rejoin at the far side. In spite of all their efforts, the two fragments drew farther and farther apart, coiling up like the ends of a black string that has snapped under pressure.

Each fragment bellied out, twisted and then broke into dozens of smaller fragments, that were carried hither and thither aimlessly, until they finally became lost within the shifting body of the enormous crowd. Then only the round black hats of the individual priests remained in evidence, floating like tiny black flowers on the surface of the obscene flood, in which their silence and their discipline and their occult power had been drowned.

As soon as the barrier of priests had disappeared, Madden again felt a burning desire to make his way towards the General Post Office and join the insurgents. When he tried to rush northwards, however, pummeling those in his path with his fists and elbows, lack of food and the punishment he had received took effect on him. He was utterly exhausted by the time he had advanced a few yards through the shifting mass.

He dropped his head on his chest and let himself be carried, limp and unresisting, hither and thither aimlessly by the shouting horde.

3

Ⅎⅎⅎⅎⅎⅎⅎⅎⅎⅎⅎⅎⅎⅎⅎⅎ

SUDDENLY there was a cry of terror:
"Here come the Lancers."

There was a moment of tense silence, during which the clatter of hoofs became distinctly audible. Then the cry of terror was repeated by hundreds of voices.

"The Lancers are coming."

With a wild rolling shout, the vast crowd stampeded like a herd of frightened cattle. Their cries rose high above the thunderous undertone of their running feet, as they fled into the side streets and to the north of the Nelson Pillar. Then the sharp clatter of steel-shod hoofs became distinct, piercing the formless tumult of the vanishing mob. It quickly grew in volume as a regiment of cavalry appeared, trotting slowly northwards from the bridge, with pennants flying in the breeze and jingling accouterments gleaming in the sunlight, noble and splendid in contrast with the sordid chaos that it had replaced.

Roused to a final effort by the mass terror, Madden fled up the street at full speed. Mrs. Colgan gripped him by the arm as he crossed the mouth of Henry Street, by the northern end of the General Post Office. She was now completely out of her wits with fright.

"My Tommy is lost now," she said. "The lads on horseback will kill him."

37

Madden was so glad to see her again that he picked her up in his arms and fondled her like a child.

"Have no fear now, good woman," he shouted as he ran with her into Upper O'Connell Street. "I'll take care of you."

After going a short distance, he turned into the deep doorway of a bank and set her down. Hardly able to keep her feet, she leaned against the door and let her head droop. He shouted a few more words of encouragement at her and then peered southwards at the advancing cavalry, round the corner of the doorway.

The head of the column was now trotting past the Metropole Hotel. The beauty of its rhythm, as it moved calmly northwards through the silent empty street, made the rattle of machine-gun fire in the distance seem unreal. Each section of the handsome bay horses advanced in a perfect line, with their proud necks arched and the sunlight rippling along their voluptuous, well-groomed haunches. Holding their lean bodies rigid above the hips, the riders rose and fell in their saddles like pistons moving back and forth within the belly of a machine. The delicate jingle of their spurs came tinkling through the sharp clatter of hoofs. Their sunburned faces wore the inscrutable and detached expression that comes from military discipline. In their hard cold eyes, that stared fixedly straight ahead over the bobbing ears of their chargers, there was no apprehension of the danger that confronted them.

Unlike his troopers, the commanding officer sat loose in his saddle and carried his service cap perched rakishly on the side of his head, as he rode out in front of the column. He glanced from side to side of the street, with a vague smile of contempt on his handsome face. When he came abreast of the General Post Office, however, he stiffened like a cat that has sighted prey. His pale blue eyes narrowed as he looked at the flags that fluttered in the breeze from the two poles at the corners of the roof and at the rude barricades in the broken windows on the ground floor. He continued to stare fixedly at the silent building as he rode past it, rising and falling rhythmically, with taut hips, like a gymnast at exercise, above his shining horse.

Madden became more and more tense as the horsemen approached. Their weapons, their uniforms, their shining accouterments, their noble chargers and their commander's arrogant face aroused the base fear of alien authority that centuries of slavery had engrained in his soul. Robbed of his manhood by that fear, he wanted terribly to flee. Yet he was unable to move. Like a rabbit that stands hypnotized by a weasel's deadly stare, an attraction that was stronger than his inherited fear held him motionless. He could hardly breathe under the strain and had to keep his mouth wide open in order to do so. His eyes became bloodshot. The wild beating of his heart, the clatter of hoofs and Mrs. Colgan's tremulous voice, at prayer behind him in the doorway, became louder and louder in his ears with each passing second.

Then a shout came from the General Post Office when the cavalry commander was trotting past the mouth of Henry Street.

"Fire!"

Madden leaped from the ground as the insurgents poured a volley from their rifles, at point-blank range, into the ranks of the advancing cavalry. His abject fear changed at once into frenzied joy. He took off his cap and swung it above his head, while the shrieks of wounded creatures mingled with the continued rattle of gunfire.

"Hurrah!" he shouted at the top of his voice.

39

"Mother of God!" cried Mrs. Colgan, as she slipped down onto her rump by the foot of the door. "Protect my little son. Don't let them take his life."

Again and again the insurgents fired at the horses and men that now spread over the thoroughfare without order or dignity, like a troop of toy soldiers sent rolling across the floor of a playroom by the foot of a sulky boy. Some horses lay on the ground, writhing in their death agony. Others lurched wildly to and fro, neighing in terror as they sprinkled the roadway with their blood. Dead and wounded troopers lay among the fallen brutes. The others had drawn their rifles but were unable to use them, being hampered by the effort to control their mounts that struggled to escape.

"Hurrah! Hurrah! Hurrah!" Madden continued to shout frantically, as he waved his cap above his head.

Realizing the blunder that he had committed, the cavalry commander drew his sword and galloped back among his scattered men, calling on them to retire. His face remained as contemptuous under fire as it had been when he trotted north at the head of his column. His bravery mitigated the consequences of his folly. The troopers rallied under the influence of his soldierly bearing and of his calm voice. Those who were still in the saddle rode with him towards the south, re-forming ranks after they had passed the O'Connell Monument. The unhorsed fled on foot, or else climbed up behind the saddles of their comrades. The dead and wounded were abandoned. So were the riderless horses, which galloped in all directions, with trailing reins and flapping stirrup leathers.

One of the horses, with a wounded trooper on his back, ran past the Nelson Pillar into Upper O'Connell Street.

The trooper rolled from the saddle as he passed the door-way in which Madden stood. He dropped his rifle as he fell. His right foot caught in the stirrup and he was dragged along the ground for about two hundred yards. Then his entangled foot came loose and he lay still on the roadway, with his battered face upturned and his limp arms out-stretched.

Madden ran to the rifle, picked it up and hurried back to the doorway. There he stood still for nearly a minute, staring at the weapon that he held out in front of his chest.

"Blood'n'ounds!" he whispered at length. "It's a soldier's rifle."

Then his exhaustion returned. He grew faint and lost his balance. He staggered backwards until he struck the door. His legs shot out from under him and he slithered to the ground beside Mrs. Colgan, who had collapsed when the firing started. He sat motionless for a little while with his eyes closed. Then he sighed deeply, opened his eyes and looked at the rifle that lay across his lap.

"A soldier's rifle!" he muttered drowsily.

He began to stroke the smoothly varnished woodwork of the stock with the tips of his fingers. He touched the bolt, the trigger guard, the magazine and the sights, like a child caressing a new toy.

"A soldier's rifle!" he whispered again and again.

Then he shuddered with sensuous delight as he recalled the poet's voice. He closed his eyes once more and let his head fall onto his left shoulder. As he lay that way, with his back to the door and the rifle across his lap, the beauti-ful images coursed through his mind, like gay white clouds dancing across the sunlit sky on a summer day, giving him exquisite pleasure.

41

4

MRS. COLGAN groaned and put her hand to her forehead. Then she caught Madden by the shoulder.

"What happened?" she said.

He opened his eyes, looked at her and smiled. His bloodied face looked grotesque, distorted by his broad grin.

"What's that?" he drawled.

"Did the lads on horseback take the Post Office?" she said.

"They took nothing," he answered drowsily.

"Did they kill our lads?" she said.

"They killed nobody," he answered. "They never fired a shot."

She stared at him fiercely, shook him and cried:

"Don't lie to a poor mother."

"Arrah! Have sense, woman," he said. "Listen to our lads singing. Would they be singing if they were killed or taken?"

She cocked her ears and listened.

"They are singing all right," she muttered.

"If you don't believe me," he said, raising his voice, "go on out and have a look at the other lads. They are lying dead on the road."

"Thank God and His Blessed Mother," she said, crossing herself.

"Go on out," he shouted. "You'll see the horse boys lying in the dust of the road, with ne'er a stir out of them."

She rose and went on tiptoe to the corner of the doorway. She shuddered and again crossed herself after she had peered towards the south.

"God have mercy on their souls," she said.

"Are you satisfied now, good woman?" he said.

Some of the insurgents were already out on the roadway, collecting the arms and equipment of their fallen enemies. Those within the General Post Office were singing.

"Ah, the poor boys!" Mrs. Colgan said with tears in her eyes. "The lovely young boys, killed in their prime! Many is the poor mother that will tear her hair when news of this terrible day is brought to her. Many is the poor child that will be left without a father, same as my Tommy was left. Ah, the poor horses! Musha, it was a shame to kill the poor dumb creatures that had done no wrong and they only going where they were ridden."

She wiped her eyes with a corner of her shawl and then turned towards Madden. She started when she saw him caress the rifle with a broad grin of delight on his face. She took a pace towards him and then halted. She stood watching him in silence for several moments. Her eyes narrowed.

"What's that thing you've got?" she said at length.

"It's a soldier's rifle," he answered without looking at her.

A cunning expression came into her eyes. She stood watching him in silence for another little while. Then she came over and squatted on her heels beside him.

"Where did you get it, sonny?" she said in a wheedling tone.

. 43

"Out in the street," he said.

"Oh! Isn't it a beauty?" she said. "Isn't it the rich thing?"

"Why wouldn't it be?" he said. "It's a soldier's rifle. It's straight from the factory."

"Oh! The richness of it!" she said, as she thrust forward her left hand and touched the stock with the tips of her fingers. "Look at the lovely wood that's in it. It must be worth a fortune."

"Everything that's in it, good woman," he said, "is the best that money can buy."

She again watched him intently for a few moments, with a cunning look in her eyes. Then she suddenly gripped his shoulder and began to speak rapidly, with tremendous energy.

"With a lovely gun like that in your fist," she said, "you can go and join the lads in the Post Office. 'Faith, you can. They'll be glad to have a fine man like yourself, with that rich and powerful gun in your fist. 'Faith, General Pearse himself, God bless him, will come and shake you by the hand. So will General Connolly. Sure, they'd have to travel a long way before they could find your equal. Didn't I see you fight like a hero? You have the fighting drop in you all right. What's your name, sonny? I didn't have time to ask you before now."

"Bartly Madden is my name," he said. "I'm from near the village of Carna."

"Madden, is it?" she cried.

She leaned back, put her palms to her lips and then threw something imaginary out upon the air; a gesture that denoted boundless enthusiasm.

"Musha, you can hold your head high with a name like that," she shouted. "Arrah! There is no better name in the whole of Connemara. Sure, the Maddens were always great fighting men. Didn't they take the sway in every fight . . . ?"

"Don't keep talking to me about fighting, good woman," he interrupted.

His voice had suddenly become shrill and thin, like that of an excited girl.

"Musha, darling," she said humbly, "sure I was only praising your kindred, I meant no harm at all."

"I couldn't fight my own shadow this minute," he shouted in the same shrill tone. "I'm half dead with the hunger. I didn't eat anything since last Saturday morning. I'm after falling out of my standing, good woman, I declare to God, I fell down here a minute ago, like a man earning his death."

"God forgive me, Bartly," she cried solicitously, "for not noticing how it was with you. Arrah! Musha, my darling Bartly, I'm the very person that will soon cure your hunger. Come on home with me now and I'll give you a dinner fit for a bishop. You poor creature! Look at the blood on your face and on your clothes. Come on home with me this minute. I'll clean your face and your clothes. You need a shave as well. Leave it to me, Bartly. I'll make you as fit and proper as a prince before you go talking to General Pearse. Rise up, treasure, and come on away with me out of here. It's no distance at all to where I live."

She dragged him to his feet without ceremony. Indeed, she handled him with almost brutal roughness, in spite of her protestations of love for him.

"Step out now, darling," she cried, when she had got him to his feet. "I'll soon put new life into you."

He halted when they had reached the corner of the door-way and looked at her anxiously.

45

"What about my rifle?" he said. "If I'm seen making off with it . . ."

"Give it to me," she interrupted briskly. "I'll put it under my dress. Then nobody will see it."

She began to push the rifle up under her smock, with the muzzle pointing towards her chin.

"Not that way," he cried in alarm. "Woman alive! It's loaded. Lord save us! It might go off and kill you stone dead. Put the butt end of it in first."

When the rifle was hidden, she clasped the butt against her left breast within her shawl. Then she took him by the arm and led him out into the street. He was very unsteady on his feet. He halted again after he had gone a few yards and began to tell her in a shrill thin voice, that sounded terribly unreal coming from such a powerfully built man, about having lost his money. She stood listening to him with manifest impatience for a little while and then abruptly cut him short.

"Never mind now, Bartly," she said, as she tried to drag him forward by tugging at his right arm with both hands. "It's in a man's nature to do foolish things. Sure, what's the good of crying about spilt milk?"

He resisted her like a stubborn goat.

"I had enough to pay my way into a farm of land," he shouted, "a farm that I had my eye on for a long time. My Uncle Patch had already put in a word for the daughter of the man that owns it. 'Faith, I was as welcome there as the flowers in May. Both father and daughter were agreeable. All I had to do was carry home the money and the match would be made in a fortnight. Ah! Lord God! If I had only gone straight home . . ."

The little woman made a supreme effort and dragged

46

him forward at that moment, interrupting his lamentation.

"What do you care now?" she cried, as they advanced unsteadily towards the corner of Henry Street, jostling one another like a pair of topers. "I know for certain that you'll be able to get into the Post Office. Then you can have revenge on the thieves that took your money and you'll be able to strike a blow for old Ireland into the bargain. Have no fear. You'll get back every penny of your money. General Pearse will see to that. Arrah! Why wouldn't he? Sure, nothing'll be too good for a hero like yourself. You'll get more besides what you lost. Won't the whole country be for the taking of yourself and your likes? You can name your own blood-money when the fight is over. Ah, my darling Bartly, you'll be a great comfort to me, when you are in there, fighting alongside my Tommy. You'll look after him, sonny. I know you will. He's all I have in the world. You won't let any harm come to him. The poor lad is so young and delicate that he can't fend for himself yet like a proper man. Oh! I have great faith in your strength and courage. It was the Mother of God herself that sent you across my path."

Madden halted once more after they had turned westwards into Henry Street, to shout about his loss in a shrill girlish voice.

"It took me eighteen months to earn it," he lamented, "working night and day. I never tasted a drop in all that time. Lord God! I often went without my supper, trying to save every penny. Then I threw it all away on the journey home. All I had to do . . ."

"Never mind now," she interrupted. "You'll get it all back, man."

"I had only to put the hundred and fifty down on the

47

table," he wailed, "and the farm was mine. Every blade of grass and grain of earth in it belonged to me. The girl was mine as well. She is as fine a girl . . . "

At that moment she managed to set him in motion by a supreme effort. They both almost fell as he lurched forward, carrying her along in front of him.

"You'll get every pennyworth out of their hides," she cried, when she had steadied herself. "It's well known that revenge is sweeter than the honey of kings."

"There's over twenty acres in the farm," he shouted, "and there's not a yard of it that isn't fit to grow a good crop. There's enough grass on it for a cow and a horse and a good few sheep."

"There's nothing lost, man," she said. "When you go home a hero, you can have any farm you want. You won't be beholden to anybody."

"God blast it! Woman," he cried, "you wouldn't see a finer girl than Barbara on the fair green of Galway, the biggest day of the year."

"Arrah! You'll have lashings of women," she said. "You'll have your pick of them."

"There was a fine hooker as well," he said, "going with the place; as fine a boat as ever sailed down Kilkerrin Bay. I'd be as strong a man as any in the West, on land and sea."

"So you will be," she said. "You'll be stronger than any man in the West when you go home a hero. Arrah! Man alive, there won't be a girl or a farm from Clifden to Maam Cross that you can't have for the lifting of your little finger. There will be ballads written about you and sold on every fair green from Westport to Loughrea."

They continued to shout in this way as they staggered westwards along the center of the street. Anger had now restored some of Madden's strength, so that his stride be-gan to lengthen. Impeded by the rifle and the tightness of her smock, Mrs. Colgan had to trot in order to keep pace with him.

Ghoulish creatures hurried eastwards across their path, carrying sacks, pushing wheelbarrows, dragging handcarts and perambulators. Their wild eyes stared hungrily from their gaunt faces towards the tumult in O'Connell Street.

5

ЛЛЛЛЛЛЛЛЛЛЛЛЛЛЛЛЛЛЛЛЛ

SHE TOOK HIM to a narrow street of two-storied red-brick tenement houses, a short distance to the northwest of the General Post Office. The tumult in O'Connell Street was clearly audible there. A heavy sweetish smell polluted the air, coming from the Moore Street slaughterhouses to the east.

In normal times the street was crowded with merry-makers at this hour of a fine holiday afternoon. A large school of men played toss halfpenny on the vacant lot to the rear of the corner public house. Many smaller groups of men and boys squatted on the pavements, playing cards for penny stakes. The roadway was full of screaming children. The little boys played marbles, spun tops and kicked balls with their bare feet. The girls played jackstones and leaped one-legged across rude squares they had chalked on the concrete. The old men leaned from the open windows of the upper stories, smoking their pipes contentedly as they chatted to their cronies across the way. The women sat knitting by the lower windows, whose lace curtains they pulled aside now and again to shout warnings at the children.

Today the place was deserted, except for a yellow mongrel bitch that lay stretched out on her side in the center of the roadway, with three black and white pups sucking at her paps. The whole population had gone east to O'Connell Street.

Even so, Mrs. Colgan locked her door and pulled the curtains carefully across the windows of the two little rooms she occupied on the ground floor of her tenement house, after she and Madden had entered. Having hidden the dead Lancer's rifle under the mattress in her bedroom, she hurried back to the kitchen and took from a cupboard the small flask of brandy that she kept there for emergencies. She poured some of the spirits into a teacup, which she offered to Madden.

"Throw that back like a good man," she said, "while I kindle the fire. Then you can sit at your ease by the hearth warming yourself. I'll have your dinner ready in three shakes of a lamb's tail."

Madden looked all round him after having swallowed the brandy. The tiny kitchen was as clean and tidy as a new pin. Not a single speck of dust tarnished the white deal table, the red chairs, Tommy's closed settle-bed to the right of the bedroom door, the lace curtains on the windows, the brown dressers laden with shining crockery and the whitewashed walls that were almost entirely covered with religious pictures.

"It's not a fire or a dinner I want," he shouted in the peculiar shrill tones of nervous exhaustion, as he stumbled across the floor towards the settle-bed, "but a place to lie down."

"Hush! Darling," she whispered anxiously, "don't talk so loud. The less the neighbors know the better."

"Arrah! What do I care?" he cried, throwing himself down flat on his back above the closed settle-bed. "All I want in God's world at this moment, good woman, is to . . ."

He stopped speaking, let his mouth fall wide open and began to breathe in the slow strong rhythm of profound sleep.

"All right, darling," she said softly.

She threw a cloth across his loins and added:

"Rest yourself there in God's name, seeing that it's sleep you need most."

Still wearing the little white-feathered black hat, she rekindled the fire on the open hearth and prepared a huge meal of boiled bacon, cabbage and potatoes in their jackets. When it was laid out on the table, together with a jug of fresh buttermilk, she went to the settle-bed and took Madden by the shoulder.

"Come on now, Bartly," she cried, shaking him vigorously. "Up and at it like a good man."

It was no use shaking him. She had to pinch his ears as hard as she could and squeeze his nostrils before he opened his eyes. Then the savory smell of the steaming food watered his palate and made him sniff hungrily. He rolled from the settle, staggered over to the table and began to eat voraciously.

She kept shouting at him, urging him to make a supreme effort, just as if he were engaged in a contest.

"Don't leave a morsel of that now," she cried. "Empty that plate quickly, so that I can fill it again for you. Thank God, there's plenty of food in the house. Stop picking at it like a bird. Throw it back, man. You had big talk about your hunger. Don't insult my house by nibbling like a dainty girl."

She refilled his plate three times before his appetite was

52

sated. Then he let his head fall heavily forward over his crossed arms and relapsed into sleep.

"Ah! You poor lad!" she cried as she ran to the settle-bed. "You were on your last legs, on account of all the fighting and drinking you had done."

Having opened the settle and turned back the clothes on the bed, which was already made, she gripped him under the armpits and dragged him across the floor with great difficulty. The sturdy little creature looked exactly like an ant that is hauling something far larger than herself, as she tugged at his supine body. She finally managed, after pausing several times for breath, to stretch him out on his back above the clothes. Then she stripped him to his shirt and bedded him.

"Sleep now," she whispered, as she tucked the blankets in all round his sides, "and let nothing come between you and the return of your strength. May God give you back all of it, darling, for it's sorely needed."

She went to a little font of holy water that hung from a nail in the wall, under a picture of the Blessed Virgin. She dipped her fingers into the water and returned to the bed on tiptoe.

"In the name of the Father, the Son and the Holy Ghost," she whispered, as she shook the drops of water from her finger tips onto his face.

Still working at great speed, she cleared the table, cleaned and pressed his suit, polished his shoes and brought him a fresh pair of socks belonging to Tommy from the clothes cupboard in her bedroom. She had found that his own socks were soiled and needed darning. Then she got an old razor that had belonged to her husband and which Tommy was beginning to use occasionally, even though his young cheeks still showed no trace of a proper beard. She lathered the sleeper's face, sharpened the blade and then drew back hesitantly when about to begin the delicate task of shaving.

"God grant he doesn't stir now and make me cut him," she whispered in a nervous tone. "Not being handy with the razor, I might give him a bad cut. Then he'd wake up mad and refuse to join the lads in the Post Office. Mother of God! Keep him quiet for me."

Her prayer was granted, for Madden lay like a corpse even while the razor passed over the bruises that the fist blows had made. It took her more than half an hour to finish shaving him. Then she washed his face, his hands and his feet. When all that was done, she felt quite exhausted and she sat down by the fire to eat a little of the dinner.

The food and a strong cup of tea revived her. She put on her spectacles and began to read a little magazine called the *Messenger of the Sacred Heart*. It contained many letters of thanksgiving, sent to the editor by sub-scribers who had received favors from various saints, in return for having special Masses said. She read all these letters with immense satisfaction several times. They gave her great spiritual comfort, because she herself had been making Novenas and paying for special Masses during the past several weeks, ever since learning that the rising was imminent. So that, in her pure and simple faith, she was convinced that Madden had been sent to her in a miraculous fashion, for the purpose of saving her son's life. The letters in the magazine, all of them from humble folk like herself, told of things that were far more extraor-dinary. Reading them banished all trace of doubt from her mind. She felt at peace.

54

Yet she got nervous when night began to fall and she could no longer read, since she was afraid to light a lamp or a candle owing to the presence of the dead Lancer's rifle under the mattress. So she put away her spectacles, went to the bed on tiptoe and stooped over the sleeper's face.

"It's time for you to wake up now, Bartly," she whispered. "Do you hear me, treasure? Night is falling. It's time for us to be going."

He lay flat on his back, with one hand thrown across his chest above the clothes, breathing as softly as a child. Food and sleep had already produced a great change in his countenance. The furrows on his forehead and the crow's-feet about the corners of his eyes had disappeared. His cheeks had filled and their skin was now as smooth as drawn silk. The only movement was a faint tremor at the curves of his nostrils with each intake of breath. In the waning light, his head seemed carved from dark marble. Her mother's heart was touched by the male beauty of his sleeping face; so that she refrained from making a serious attempt to awaken him in spite of her anxiety.

"It would be a sin," she said to herself, as she turned away from the bed. "He'll need every ounce of strength that God sees fit to give him and it's only through sleep that he can get it. Ah! The lovely boy! The woman that bore him may well be proud of her work!"

She went back to the hearth, took her rosary beads from a hook in the wall, crossed herself and began to recite the first decade, swaying gently from side to side. She had not got very far with the recital when she jumped to her feet again, startled by the explosion of several grenades in the distance.

"Jesus, Mary and Joseph!" she cried.

She put her beads back on the hook and ran to the bed. Now she was furiously angry with Madden for lying there asleep while her son was in danger. She pulled back the clothes rudely and shouted at him.

"Wake up, man," she cried. "Do you hear me? They are shooting again with the fall of night."

The hand that had lain across his chest slipped down to his side when the clothes were drawn from under it. That was all the movement he made in response to her cries. He continued to breathe like a child in profound sleep.

"Shame on you," she cried, "for lying there asleep while my Tommy needs you. I heard terrible blasting just now. Up with you, man."

As he continued to sleep, she threw herself upon him with violence and thumped him on the chest with her fists. He groaned, thrust out his arms drowsily and pushed her aside. She was thrown back several feet. By the time she returned to the attack, he had turned towards the wall and crossed his arms over his stomach. His breathing was now loud and hoarse.

"What am I to do with him?" she cried petulantly, as she tugged at his shoulders, trying to pull him away from the wall. "He's dead to the world."

She suddenly abandoned her hold and rushed about the kitchen, wringing her hands and gabbling incoherently. Then she went to the window, pulled aside the curtain and peered into the street. There was nobody in sight. Still gabbling, she ran to the mantelpiece, took down a candle and lit it at the fire. She picked up a stout cudgel from the fuel cupboard and returned to the bed, still running.

"Up with you now," she cried in a savage tone, as she

56

whacked Madden's curved back with the cudgel. "Be quick about it, too, or I won't leave an inch of skin on your backside. I didn't feed you and slave for you just to let you lie there, like a slothful coward, while brave lads are dying for Ireland. Up with you or I'll have your life. 'Faith, I'm the woman for blackguards like you."

He began to whimper as she continued to strike him. Then he grunted and rolled onto his back. He stopped breathing for a few moments. Finally he opened his eyes and looked at her in astonishment. Thereupon she lowered the cudgel and held the lighted candle close to his face.

"Ha!" she cried in triumph, panting as a result of her violent effort. "It was a hard job waking you. I never saw such a shameless creature. Up with you now, or I'll begin again."

He closed his eyes once more, yawned and stretched himself to his full length.

"Don't you dare do that," she screamed. "I dare you to fall asleep again. If you do, I'll put murder on my soul. Night is falling, man alive, and there's terrible blasting over there beyond."

Madden growled and pushed the lighted candle away from his face. He opened his eyes and looked at her sourly, licking his lips and making grimaces like a person that has swallowed something unpleasant.

"Who are you, good woman?" he said at length.

His deep gruff voice was strangely different from the girlish tone of his exhaustion.

"Who am I?" she cried in indignation, as she stepped back and dropped the cudgel to the floor. "Arrah! Bad cess to you! Have you no shame at all in you? I've been tending you like a mother for hours. Now you ask me who I am?"

Putting her hand on her hip, she upbraided him with violence. He listened to her with interest for a little while. Then he yawned, scratched his head and stretched himself luxuriously. Finally, he sat up on his haunches and struck his chest with both fists.

"Where are my clothes, good woman?" he said.

She stopped gabbling, took in a deep breath and smiled.

"Thanks be to God," she said. "You're in your proper senses at last. That's the talk, sonny. There they are on the chair, darling, all ready for you. Up with you now. It's time for us to be going. Night is falling and I heard great blasting just now."

He looked at her with hostility and said:

"Where would we be going?"

"To the General Post Office, man," she cried. "Aren't you going to join the rising? Didn't I promise to take you to General Pearse?"

"You're talking to the wrong man, good woman," he said, as he leaped briskly to the floor.

She crossed herself in fright.

"Lord save us!" she said. "What's that you're after saying?"

He took his trousers from the chair and pulled them on hurriedly.

"You're talking to the wrong man," he repeated. "You're making a big mistake if you think I'm going to any such place with you."

She took two short steps towards him and held the lighted candle close to his face. Then she peered at him intently, as if trying to make sure of his identity.

"You don't mean what you say, treasure," she whispered.

He buttoned his braces, sat down on the chair and began to pull on the pair of fresh socks she had given him.

"I mean every word of it, good woman," he said. "I've learned sense and I paid dearly for learning it. I paid a hundred and fifty pounds of hard-earned money for the sense that's now in my head. So don't be talking to me about making a worse fool of myself. You're talking to the wrong man."

"Shame on you!" she cried in rage. "Was it how you turned coward in your sleep?"

"Never mind that talk," he said coldly. "I can be as deaf as a stone when I don't want to hear. You've been good-natured and obliging. You need have no fear that I'll walk out of your house and forget what you've done for me. I have a few pounds put away in the bank, from the season I fished in a Galway nobby before going to England. As soon as I get back home, I'll send you a hansel for . . ."

"You barbarian!" she cried. "Are you offering to pay for what was given to you in God's name?"

He paused in the act of tying his shoelaces and said:

"I'm in your house, so I forgive you for calling me a barbarian. All the same, good woman, an insult was never before cast in the face of a man of my breed without . . ."

"Musha, may God forgive me as well," she said humbly, "for speaking to you from the bitterness of my heart. The words passed my lips unknown to me, driven out by the sorrow of a widowed mother, whose only son is fighting without a man of his blood to stand by him in the gap of danger."

He got to his feet and said:

"May God protect him! It's my hearty prayer. However,

it's every man for himself, in this world. Would you kindly give me a basin of water to wash my face, good woman?"

"I will and welcome," she said. "I'll give you water and a towel to dry yourself."

After she had done so, she stood watching him for a little while with the same cunning expression in her eyes as when she had seen him caress the rifle in the doorway of the bank. Then she went on tiptoe into her bedroom, took the rifle from beneath the mattress, put it behind her back and returned to the kitchen. There she stood with her back to the wall near the settle-bed, watching him intently. Her eyes had now narrowed to slits. Her little pinched face looked very cruel.

When Madden had washed himself and finished dressing, he stood by the table with his cap held in front of his chest and bowed to her. Now it was hard to believe he was the same man that had lounged between two pillars of the portico at noon, destitute and forlorn. With his clothes cleaned and pressed, his face shaved, his shoes polished and his strength restored, he looked very strong and resolute. His close-cropped fair hair stood up like bristles on his skull.

"I'm on my way now, good woman," he said in the ceremonious tone of a departing guest. "So I'm asking God to keep sickness and misfortune from your door and to bless you and everybody that belongs to you."

She curtseyed to him and replied:

"The same to you, good man. Forgive me for the poverty of my house and for the inhospitable way I treated you."

Then she suddenly brought the rifle from behind her back, rushed over to him and said:

"You were forgetting this."

He stared in surprise at the weapon that she held out before him. He had completely forgotten, since waking, the ecstasy of its possession in the doorway of the bank.

"Take it," she cried fiercely, as she thrust it at his chest. "It was God put it in your way. He has a good reason for everything He does. You can't go without it. Take it in your hands and may you be worthy of it."

He put on his cap and took the rifle from her slowly. He shuddered as he gripped it.

"Blood'n'ounds!" he muttered hoarsely.

As soon as he touched the weapon, the Idea again entered his mind and sent his blood coursing wildly through his veins. This time, however, it did not bring in its train the images of romantic longing that had previously given him such pleasure. Instead, he now recalled how the soldiers had fallen and how the wounded horses had neighed in terror as they sprinkled the roadway with their blood.

Seeing that her ruse had succeeded, she crossed herself in gratitude and moved away from him on tiptoe. She went to the hearth and heaped ashes on the fire. Then she brought a jug of water from the sink and doused the hot ashes, making them sizzle and smoke.

"We had a rifle in our place," Madden cried out in a loud and arrogant tone, while she was putting away the jug. "It was two years ago, when John Redmond's crowd was drilling there. A man that used to be a corporal in the Connaught Rangers taught us how to fire it. 'Faith, it was a fine gun all right, but you couldn't compare it with this one. Ah! Lord God! This one is a beauty. The rifle we had in our place was old and you had to take aim with it a little to one side, even when there was hardly any wind at all. I was getting to be able for it, though, when the parish priest stopped the drilling. Arrah! This rifle takes the sway from all the guns I ever saw. You can see it's straight from the factory. Blood'n'ounds! I bet you could hit a wren with this one at two hundred yards on a clear day?"

"It's time for us to be going now, sonny," she said gently, as she put on her shawl. "Night has fallen."

She brought holy water from the font.

"With a rifle like this," Madden shouted, while she sprinkled the weapon, "you could kill the strongest beast that ever walked."

Then she sprinkled his forehead and said:

"Stop talking now, darling, and let us go."

He was so excited that he crossed himself without taking off his cap. Then he slung the rifle across his left shoulder and strode to the door.

"Lead the way now," he shouted, "to wherever there is fighting."

6

Nɪɢʜᴛ ʜᴀᴅ ꜰᴀʟʟᴇɴ. The sound of gunfire had subsided. The silence of peace lay over the city, except for the area adjoining the General Post Office. There the looting mob was making carnival.

As Madden and Mrs. Colgan debouched into Henry Street and turned eastwards towards the Nelson Pillar, they came upon the pillagers.

"Oh! Lord God!" cried Mrs. Colgan. "Look at the ruffians. Have they no shame in them at all? They're making off like hungry dogs with whatever they can find."

Like an army of marauding ants that had come across rich spoil, ragged slum dwellers were going back and forth along the street in never-ending lines. Those going west were laden with all they could carry on their persons, or in rude vehicles they had improvised. They glanced furtively from side to side as they hastened, fearful that their booty might be snatched from them before they reached home. Those going empty towards the east looked fixedly straight ahead, their eyes ablaze with greed.

Mrs. Colgan kept shaking her fists at them, as she shouted in a tone of violent indignation:

"Don't ye know that ye are bringing shame on our country? Ye are the scum of the earth sure enough. It's a wonder the ground doesn't open up and swallow ye. Ho! Ho! God will punish ye with hell's fire for this awful robbery."

Her indignation was largely simulated. As an honest and God-fearing person, she was certainly opposed to looting. Nevertheless, her angry shouting was inspired by fear that Madden might be tempted to join the pillagers, in order to recoup himself for the loss of his money. If he did so, she knew that he would abandon all idea of joining the insurgents and that she would lose the "miraculous protector" sent by the Blessed Virgin for her son.

Her fear was groundless. Like a lover in the first flush of a newborn passion, he was utterly indifferent to the presence of the creatures that dodged from his path. He never even glanced at one of them, as he marched with his head thrown far back and a look of rapture in his fierce blue eyes, pounding the roadway as if it were a living enemy. His mind was bereft of thought; but his whole being was intensely conscious of the weapon that he carried. Its touch gave him a marvelous sense of power and dignity.

A soldier's rifle! He was carrying a soldier's rifle through the streets of Dublin, without having to wear the hated uniform of the imperial oppressor, that had kept his kindred disarmed and enslaved for centuries. There in front of him lay the Nelson Pillar, the towering symbol of imperial power. He was marching straight towards it, carrying this beautiful weapon that he had taken from an imperial soldier. Such an astounding and glorious fact was beyond the realm of thought. It could only be felt through the blood, like the sensual possession of a beloved one. It was more intoxicating than the strongest liquor.

When he was within fifty yards of the towering monu-

64

ment, however, he was jolted from the enjoyment of his rapture by coming into contact with a dense mob of people that were looting four large shops. There the roadway was almost completely blocked. Very few of these pillagers were serious folk, that made off to their homes when laden. The great majority were making merry on the spot with their booty. The foolish creatures even threw away articles of great value that did not make an immediate appeal to their sensual appetites. The ground was littered with abandoned merchandise, through which the pillagers lurched drunkenly to and fro, wearing fantastic new garments over their rags, shouting and singing, like revelers at a macabre fair.

In great fear, Mrs. Colgan clung to the back of his jacket with both hands as he began to force a passage with his fists through this mob. Her voice became shrill and strident, urging him to resist temptation.

"Never mind these dirty people, Bartly," she cried. "In every country there are scoundrels, who have no respect for the laws of God or man. Be on your way, sonny, and pay no heed to them. Thieves and scavengers have disgraced every cause, no matter how noble. You have better work to do than thievery. There is a far greater reward in store for you than a few miserable things snatched from a shop. I'm telling you, darling love, that God's blessed treasure will be poured into your lap when the fight is over. You'll go home a conquering hero to the West, with a bag full of gold on your back. Ho! Ho! The dirty villains! I spit on them. Beat them out of your way. Have no mercy on them."

She could have spared herself the trouble of making these exhortations and fantastic promises. Madden never heard a word of what she said. Close contact with these lewd creatures had driven out the Idea and filled his mind with angry doubt. He felt like a man who is trying to escape from a pit swarming with reptiles, whose slimy bodies encircle his limbs. Even when he reached clear ground to the east of the mob, his rapture did not return. On the contrary, he began to be afraid of carrying the dead Lancer's rifle slung across his shoulder, as he reached the corner of the street and came abreast of the General Post Office.

Lower O'Connell Street was now almost empty, all the way from the Nelson Pillar to the bridge. There was no sign of the insurgents. The dull thud of their crowbars and sledgehammers, however, came from the interior of many buildings on either side of the street. They were tunneling an interior line of communication between the various outposts they had established on the approaches to their general headquarters.

He came to a halt at the corner and glanced southwards. The great empty space, the sinister thumping and the corpses of the cavalry horses, that still lay on the roadway where they had fallen, increased his fear.

"Lord God!" he said to himself. "What am I doing? Am I out of my mind?"

Mrs. Colgan took him by the arm and dragged him southwards along the front of the General Post Office.

"Come on now," she said. "We're nearly there, thank God."

They had reached the northern corner of the portico when she again seized his arm and called on him to halt. Then she pointed to a small group of insurgents that had just entered the thoroughfare from the lane to the south of the building.

"There's my Tommy," she whispered excitedly. "That's him wearing the uniform in the last row. We'll wait here until we see where his crowd is going."

Under the influence of the fear and doubt that were rapidly growing in his mind, Madden looked with hostility at the group of insurgents. It comprised eleven men. An officer marched in front. The others followed in two ranks. The officer and Tommy Colgan, who walked in the rear file beside a gray-haired man who wore a shabby belted raincoat, were the only ones that had a uniform of any sort. The officer strode along in fine style, very erect and haughty in his bearing, like a proper soldier. The rest of them walked with downcast heads, making no attempt to keep in step.

Their unsoldierly appearance made a very poor impression on Madden. These men were altogether unlike those that had so thrilled him at noon by their enraptured faces.

"Blood'n'ounds!" he said to himself. "Sure, even a madman wouldn't join that crowd."

Mrs. Colgan waited until she saw that the group was headed towards North Earl Street, at the far side of the Nelson Pillar. Then she took Madden's arm.

"Come on, Bartly," she said. "We'll follow him."

Madden angrily resisted her effort to drag him out into the roadway.

"Why should we follow that crowd?" he said.

"Stop talking, man," she said. "Hurry before we lose sight of him."

"I'll not move a foot," he said, "until you tell me where you are taking me."

"Come on," she shouted, tugging at his arm violently.

"My Tommy is with that crowd and we must follow him."

"Devil a foot I'll go with you," he said. "Before we left the house, you said you were taking me to General Pearse. Now you want to take me somewhere else. What's your game, good woman?"

"Never mind General Pearse," she shouted. "Aren't you the conceited man, wanting to meet the general before you have struck a proper blow? Arrah! Don't you know you have to join his army before you can meet him? Tommy is with this crowd here, so this is the crowd you'll join. Come on now and do as I tell you."

Madden glanced back over his shoulder at the General Post Office and decided to follow the little woman in order to get as far as possible away from it. The last thing in the world that he wanted to do at the moment was to meet General Pearse or strike a blow of any sort.

"Blood'n'ounds!" he cried, as he thrust aside her clutching hand and stepped out into the roadway. "You're as aggravating a person as I ever met."

She urged him to make haste, in the shrill tone of a mother bird that has seen a hawk circling overhead and is herding her young to shelter. He walked very slowly across the boulevard without paying any heed to her cries. In fact he stopped dead after he had gone less than halfway, to stare at the corpse of a cavalry horse. The animal now looked inoffensive, motionless in death and stripped of its fine accouterments. Yet it reminded him unpleasantly of the hypnotic fear he had experienced in the doorway of the bank.

"Hurry, man," she cried, thumping him in the ribs with her little hands. "We've lost sight of him."

He moved forward slowly and said to her:

"Shut up. I've had enough of your gab."

Then he glanced over his left shoulder at the enormous crowd that was making merry in Upper O'Connell Street. The whole thoroughfare was densely packed from the Pillar to the Parnell Monument. He shuddered, unslung his rifle and put it behind his back. He was now terribly afraid of being seen in possession of the beautiful weapon whose carriage had caused him to feel rapture a few minutes previously.

Mrs. Colgan noticed the gesture.

"Mother of God!" she prayed. "Keep him from turning tail at the last moment. This is a wild and uncertain class of a man that you sent me. Help me to handle him properly."

When they reached the mouth of North Earl Street, Madden halted and put his back to the wall of the shop at the southern corner. Mrs. Colgan pointed to the group of insurgents, who had halted in the middle of the roadway, a few yards to the east.

She again took Madden by the arm and said:

"There they are, Bartly. Come on over to them."

He cursed as he thrust her hand aside brutally.

"Leave me alone," he growled, "or I might lose my temper with you."

"All right, then," she said, moving away from him. "Wait here while I go and have a word with Tommy's boss."

As she hurried towards the east, she looked back over her shoulder and said to him in a menacing tone:

"If you move a foot out of there, I'll haunt you with my curses to my dying day."

Madden again looked towards Upper O'Connell Street. His eyes became fixed on two young women, who were sitting on the belly of a dead horse to the north of the Pillar, a few yards from where he stood. One of the young women was very pretty. She was neatly dressed in a white blouse, a blue serge skirt and a yellow cashmere shawl that was thrown loosely about her shoulders. She swayed from side to side, with her head thrown far back, singing at the top of her voice. The other woman was pale and thin. Her black hair was in disorder. Her soiled pink blouse was unbuttoned almost to her waist. Her red skirt was raised up far above her knees. Her gray shawl lay on the horse's rump. She sat motionless, with her head drooping and her mouth wide open, holding an open whiskey bottle by the neck with both hands between her thighs.

A street urchin of about thirteen, wearing a black silk hat and a gray frock coat that reached almost to his heels, came up behind the two women and made an obscene gesture towards them with a silver-topped cane that he bore before him in both hands.

This scene inspired Madden with such disgust and horror that he decided to escape at once from the little woman, whom he now looked upon as an agent of the devil, sent to lead him to damnation. He was about to throw away the rifle and run northwards towards the Parnell Monument when he remembered that he had stolen the weapon from a dead Lancer. He must hide it, he thought in his panic, lest it should be found and constitute evidence against him. Thereupon he turned to his right and plunged headlong through the open doorway of the shop against whose wall he had been leaning.

70

The shop was already completely gutted by the mob. The shelves were naked. The floor was littered with empty cardboard boxes. An old blindman stood a little way within the door, listening attentively with his head turned sideways. He was the beggar who had walked along the pavement at noon before the Metropole Hotel, singing to the young officers of the imperial army.

"Noreen!" he cried in a tremulous voice. "Is that you, darling?"

Madden stood within the door, put the rifle behind his back and stared at the blindman in silence.

"You're not Noreen," said the blindman, as he began to shuffle forward inch by inch through the litter, with his hands outstretched. "You have boots on you and she's barefooted. Where is she? Where is my little niece? The wicked thing! God will punish her for leaving me alone in this place."

Realizing that the old man was blind, Madden was looking about the room for a place to hide his rifle when a little girl entered at a run. She was the child who had begged from the officers while the old man sang. She now wore a fine sealskin coat over her white pinafore. It hung down to her bare feet that were black with dirt. Its wide glossy sleeves almost completely covered her tiny hands, in which she carried a pair of new shoes. Her dark eyes shone with joy as she thrust the shoes against the old man's chest.

"I got a lovely pair for you, Uncle Joe," she cried gaily. "They are the right size, too. Feel the gorgeous leather that's in them."

"'Faith, it's true for you," the blindman said in an avaricious tone as he fondled the shoes. "Merciful God!

71

Nobody ever saw the likes of them. They are as soft as silk. Oh! You can almost bend them double like a pair of gloves."

Then he lowered his voice and added:

"Take me away from here now, for fear some robber might steal them from me. There's no law or order out there in the streets and we must be very careful as we go home."

"Don't be afraid, Uncle Joe," the little girl cried joyfully, as she led him out into the street. "Sure, nobody would rob a blindman. In any case, there's plenty now for everybody."

Madden was again looking about the shop for a hiding place when Mrs. Colgan entered.

"Didn't I tell you not to stir?" she shouted angrily.

He started violently as she spoke to him. Then he looked at her with hatred. For a brief moment he was tempted to knock her unconscious, hide his weapon and take to his heels. However, the desire to do so merely sent a cold shiver down his spine. Panic had numbed his will. She now hypnotized him in the way that the advancing cavalry had done. He licked his parched lips, again slung the rifle over his left shoulder and followed her out of the shop with downcast eyes.

She halted a little to the right of the door and pointed to a heap of diverse articles that the insurgents were collecting out in the middle of the roadway.

"They are going to make a wall across the street here," she said. "The boss is gone on ahead to put two of his men on watch. We'll wait here until he comes back."

Then she leaned towards Madden, pointed to the Amiens

72

Street railway station that lay about half a mile due east and added in a confidential whisper:

"There's a crowd of soldiers over there. They've just come from the north on the train. The wall is to stop them, in case they take it into their heads to come charging at the Post Office."

This street was also densely thronged with people who were feverishly looting everything in sight. At first they paid no attention to the heap of abandoned articles being collected by the insurgents, as they hurried east and west with their loads of booty. Like ants that have come across an obstruction, they deflected their course slightly and passed on either side of the heap without looking at it. As it grew in size, however, they became interested in it. The abandoned articles, that had lain unwanted on the roadway for some time, aroused their cupidity now that others were collecting them.

Finally a tall gaunt woman, who carried a roll of blue serge cloth on her shoulder like a log, halted and stared at a table that had just been thrown on top of the heap.

"Blood'n'ounds!" she said. "It's mahogany."

She dropped the roll of cloth and seized the table.

"Leave that alone," an insurgent said to her. "We need it for our barricade."

"Kiss my arse," the woman said to him contemptuously.

The insurgent wrestled with her, trying to rescue the table; but she resisted him fiercely.

"God blast you!" she yelled. "Don't you see it's mahogany?"

Then a huge man, who wore an oil-stained suit of dungarees, appeared on the scene. He spat on his hands, hitched

73

up his trousers, felled the insurgent with a blow on the ear, sent the gaunt woman sprawling with a kick in the rump, hoisted the mahogany table onto his broad back and walked away briskly towards the east.

Thereupon, the mob fell on the heap and rapidly plundered its contents. The other insurgents rushed forward, picked up their fallen comrade and then tried to ward off the plundering crowd. Their futile efforts merely aroused the people's anger.

"Go on home out of that, you bowsie," cried a red-haired woman with huge breasts, as she spat in an insurgent's face. "Go on, you lousy little sniveler, before the soldiers come and settle your hash."

A dignified old man, who carried an expensive fur coat on his arm, shook his walking stick at the insurgents and cried:

"You have absolutely no right to interfere."

Then he leaned back, threw out his arms and added in the unnatural tone of a declaiming actor:

"Canaille!"

The insurgents retreated in a compact group to the pavement where Madden and Mrs. Colgan were standing. The jeering mob came hot in pursuit.

"Canaille!" the dignified old actor continued to shout.

Mrs. Colgan tried to push Madden forward, as she whispered urgently:

"Stand by my Tommy. There he is, the tall lad in the uniform. Don't let these rowdies hurt him."

Madden turned on her angrily and shouted:

"Arrah! Go to hell. Why doesn't the bloody fellow use his own fists?"

74

He himself was struck at that moment by a stockily built man who had mounted the pavement. He just sent the fellow reeling away into the roadway with a short kick in the stomach. Then he retreated farther back on the pavement.

The insurgent commander forced his way through the crowd a few moments later and took up position on the edge of the pavement, in front of his cowed men. He carried a Mauser pistol in his hand.

"Disperse!" he cried out to the mob in a stern tone.

He was a tall lean man of twenty-eight called Michael Kinsella, wearing the uniform of a captain in the Irish Volunteers. He had a pale ascetic face, gray eyes and brown hair that was faintly tinged with red. He looked very handsome and dignified as he calmly faced the mob.

"Blood'n'ounds!" Madden said to himself, as he stared at the newcomer. "There is a fellow that has the stuff in him."

The Idea again entered his mind and dispelled his panic. His body became tense. He gripped the strap of his rifle fiercely and edged forward towards Kinsella, at whom he stared fixedly.

The crowd, which was now growing rapidly to a great size, greeted the command to disperse with a roar of mocking laughter.

"Hello, gorgeous!" said the red-haired woman who had spat at the insurgent, as she flaunted her huge breasts in front of Kinsella and winked her left eye. "Have you anything good in your mind?"

"Doesn't he look lovely?" said another woman, who carried a laden clothes basket on top of her head. "I bet he's

75

a devil for his oats. Those solemn pale-faced lads are always the best. He can have a sup out of my pint any time he likes."

The dignified old actor brandished his walking stick and again shouted with exaggerated emphasis:

"Canaille!"

Kinsella pointed his pistol at his tormentors and cried out:

"I warn you that I shall be compelled to use force unless . . ."

His words were drowned as the mocking laughter changed to a savage roar. Those in the front ranks screamed as they tried to force their way backwards from the pistol's menace. Their escape was blocked, however, by the efforts of those in the rear to move forward and attack. So that the whole mass swayed back and forth uncertainly, like two waves that meet before a great sea wall, the one advancing with its power unspent and the other in retreat from its delivered blow.

Then a bullet-headed man, whose skull was shorn to the bone like that of a convict, raised both his arms to their full extent above the center of the mob and cried out:

"So that's the game. No sooner do the people get rid of one tyrant than another tries to take his place."

The whole roadway was now blocked to the northern pavement, along which some serious folk still bent on pillage were going east and west in furtive silence with their loads; and these collided and became entangled as they tried to pass within the confined space, like drifting wreckage in the narrows of a flooded river.

Then a wild triumphant shout came from the northern pavement, about fifteen yards to the east:

"Champagne!"

A thin little man was standing in front of a broken plate-glass window, over which the words "Aloysius J. Cassidy Brandy Merchant" were written in ornamental gold lettering. He held a magnum of champagne in both hands, high up before his face. He gazed at it in worship, like a priest holding aloft a sacred chalice. The great bottle was open and the foaming wine cascaded from its neck, drenching the little man's dirty hands and the sleeves of his ragged jacket in its fall.

"Champagne!" he cried exultantly. "I found a secret room in the cellar. It's full to the roof with champagne and brandy. There's a cartload of champagne down there."

The magic word caused those on the outskirts of the crowd to turn and run towards the foaming wine.

"Champagne!" they shouted as they ran.

Just as a flock of sea birds standing on a shore rise singly and then in ever-increasing numbers at sight of leaping fish, the attacking crowd turned in tens and scores and hundreds to charge madly towards the wine.

"Champagne! Champagne! Champagne!" they chanted.

Two elderly sisters, both wearing spectacles and belted blue overcoats, were going past the broken window to the west, carrying between them a yellow woolen blanket that was laden with white crockery, when they were struck by the charging mob. One of them lost her grip, being thrust aside by a man's swinging arm. As her end of the blanket fell, the crockery poured out onto the street, where it was smashed by the running feet. The other sister clung desper-

77

ately to her end, uttering forlorn cries as she was buffeted by those going past her. Then the loose end of the blanket was caught up and thrown about her head, while she herself was carried forward through the hole.

The thin little man had by then put the neck of the bottle to his lips and begun to drink with zest, indifferent to the shouting multitude that went past him on either side, smashing the jaggered pieces of glass that still clung to the window frame. Then the bullet-headed man with the shorn skull snatched the bottle and carried it aloft through the interior of the shop, behind the elderly woman who had the yellow blanket coiled about her head. He kept trying to drink as he was borne forward, but could not find sufficient room to lower his arm and bring the bottle's neck into contact with his lips. So that the wine poured out onto his face and his hairless skull.

Outside in the street, the lines of people going east and west with pillage were now forced to make a wide detour, in order to circumvent the mass that stood like a cluster of bees before the broken window, trying to enter the already crowded wineshop.

7

KINSELLA put his men to work as soon as the mob had gone.

"Now is our time," Mrs. Colgan said to Madden.

She stood in front of Kinsella and bowed low to him.

"Beg pardon, sir," she said. "I'd like to have a word with you."

"What is it?" said Kinsella.

She pointed towards her son.

"That's my Tommy," she said. "He's my only child. I'm Mary Anne Colgan. He's only just turned sixteen, but you'd hardly believe he's less than twenty on account of his great height. He has a fine uniform, too, which is more than the rest of your crowd can say for themselves, begging your pardon for casting at them. He paid for his uniform, 'faith, week by week, out of his wages. He paid for his rifle too. That shows you, sir, that he's a good steady lad. He's delicate, but there's iron in him, just like his father. You can take my word for it. He'll do anything you ask of him, or die in the attempt. It's not about him, though, that I want to speak to you at all. It's about this other man beside me here."

She nudged Madden in the ribs and whispered:

"Step forward, Bartly, and raise your cap to the gentleman. He's the boss over this crowd. Raise your cap and say good day politely to him, like a good man."

Madden paid no heed to her. He stood rigidly to attention, staring at Kinsella. The Idea had now found a leader for him to worship. The vague mystical longings inspired in him by the poet's words had taken flesh, in this lean man with the ascetic face and the mysterious eyes of a monk. He felt taut from head to foot like a drawn bow, as he waited to establish contact with his chosen one.

Mistaking the cause of his silence, the little woman again nudged him in the ribs.

"What's holding you?" she said. "Is it afraid you are? Raise your cap!"

Startled by having his courage impugned before his new-found leader, he took a pace forward, clicked his heels and put the forefinger of his right hand to the peak of his cap.

"I want to join your crowd, sir," he cried out in a hoarse voice.

Kinsella looked into the fierce blue eyes of the Connemara man for a few moments in silence.

"Are you a member of the Irish Volunteers or the Citizen Army?" he said at length.

A faint tremor passed down Madden's spine on being addressed by his chosen leader; he was like a newly broken colt that feels the caress of its master's hand on its neck.

"I don't belong to any crowd," he said, "but I have a rifle and I can handle it fairly well. I learned to fire it when John Redmond's crowd was drilling in our place. Then the parish priest . . ."

"Why do you want to join us?" said Kinsella.

Afraid that Madden might not give the proper answer to this question, Mrs. Colgan hurriedly intervened.

80

"It's because he has the fighting drop in him, sir," she said. "I saw him lay low more than a score of men during the day. He took that fine gun he has from one of the horseback soldiers. Arrah! Why wouldn't he be a good fighting man? His name is Bartly Madden and he comes from Connemara like myself. That's the country where they breed good fighting men. It's well known that a Connemara man would rather fight than eat his dinner, the hungriest day he ever was. It is, 'faith and what's more, there isn't a better class of fighting man from Oughterard to Letterfrack than a Madden."

Kinsella had been looking intently at Madden while she spoke. He now put his hand on the Connemara man's shoulder and said:

"All right, comrade. Give us a hand with this barricade. Later on, I'll have a talk with you."

Madden's face became radiant on hearing these words.

"Thank you, sir," he muttered hoarsely.

Mrs. Colgan was equally happy. She took Kinsella's hand and kissed it fervently.

"The blessing of God on you, sir," she said. "I know you won't regret taking him in with your crowd. You have a lad now that's worth a dozen. He'll fight from morning to night without even a drink of water."

She followed Madden over to the other insurgents, who had begun to erect a barricade on the northern pavement. She introduced him to Tommy.

"Let the two of ye stand together now in the gap of danger," she cried. "Let ye defend one another through thick and thin. I'm a happy woman now, Tommy, knowing that Bartly is with you. He'll look after you."

Tommy scowled in answer to Madden's nod.

"I don't want anybody to look after me," he said in a surly tone. "I can take care of myself."

"None of that now," said Madden to the lad, as he slung his rifle across his back. "Don't be impertinent to your mother."

He was again fond of the little woman, whom he had been tempted to knock unconscious a short time previously. It was through her agency that he had found his leader.

The little woman raised her clasped hands up in front of her face.

"Blessed Mother of God!" she whispered with fervor. "You have answered my prayer. I bow low before your holy name."

Then she threw her shawl far back on her shoulders, put her hands on her hips and cried out in a hearty tone:

"I'm going to get ye bite and sup now, lads. Ye'll need nourishment by the time ye have finished that big wall. I won't be long gone. I know where to get bread and meat."

Thereupon, she made off towards the Nelson Pillar, trotting minutely within the tapering circuit of her white smock. She halted as she passed the dead horse on which the two young women were sitting. She again raised her clasped hands before her face and gave thanks to the Blessed Virgin with great fervor, for having sent Madden to be her son's "miraculous protector."

Then she trotted westwards out of sight.

8

THE BARRICADE stretched three quarters of the way across the street when the mob came out of the wineshop in a state of wild intoxication. They headed westwards, led by the man with the shorn skull, singing in discordant chorus.

Pistol in hand, Kinsella stepped forward to confront them. He pointed towards the open channel by the northern pavement when the man with the shorn skull was five yards away.

"Keep moving," he said.

The man with the shorn skull was now naked to the waist, except for a narrow strip of white cotton shirt that clung to his left shoulder. He had a bottle of brandy in each hand. He bore down on Kinsella with his head thrust forward and his biceps flexed. When he was only two yards away, however, the pistol and Kinsella's steady glance made him deflect his course. He headed for the open channel to the north. He again took courage as he was skirting the barricade. With a savage cry, he struck at Madden with the bottle that he carried in his right hand. Madden was crouching at that moment over a chest of drawers that he was placing in the barricade. The bottle just missed his head. He straightened himself and promptly felled the shorn brute.

83

Seeing their leader fall, the other drunkards came shuffling to a halt and stared in wonder at the wall being built by the insurgents whom their lawless power had herded on the pavement like frightened sheep a short time previously. They felt cowed by this appearance of order and discipline among the chaos in which they had been joyously rioting.

Then a few score of those in the front ranks marched in silence through the open channel to the west, without glancing at the shorn brute, who lay face downwards in the gutter, clutching a still unbroken brandy bottle in his outstretched left hand. The rest of them remained behind and began to sing snatches of patriotic songs and begged for arms, saying they wanted to fight for their freedom.

The barricade had reached the edge of the northern pavement when a young woman came running round the corner of Lower O'Connell Street in a state of great excitement.

"I've great news, lads," she shouted.

She was dressed in the dark green uniform of the women's corps attached to the Irish Volunteers. She was tall and robust, with square shoulders and narrow hips, that swayed rhythmically as she advanced with long strides like a man. Her head was bare and her luxuriant black hair was in disorder. Her wild blue eyes were bloodshot.

On reaching the barricade, she put her hands on her hips, threw back her head and cried out in a voice that was shrill with hysteria:

"I've just come from the South Dublin Union, where our lads have routed over two thousand of the enemy."

Both the insurgents and the mob raised a mighty cheer on hearing this news. Hats and caps were thrown into the air. Madden was on the point of raising a shout when he saw Kinsella come round the barricade, going towards the young woman. Noticing that his leader's face showed no trace of excitement, he restrained himself. Under the influence of the Idea, he wanted to imitate the man who was now his master, in every possible way.

"We had only seventy men there," the young woman continued, when the cheering had subsided. "Half of them were down after three hours of fierce fighting. The rest were cornered in a few rooms of the Union Hospital, with the enemy charging at them. Then Cathal Brugha saved the day. Riddled with bullets from the waist down, he was kneeling in a pool of his own blood by the kitchen window, firing his revolver at the enemy until his ammunition was spent. Then he crossed himself with his empty gun and began to sing 'God Save Ireland.' That did the trick. The other lads rallied and began to sing with him. Then they charged and swept the enemy off his feet. Our flag still flies over the South Dublin Union. Up Cathal Brugha! God Save Ireland!"

Like thunder re-echoing along a mountainside, a great cheer swept down the street towards the east.

"God Save Ireland!" roared the crowd.

The young woman then turned to Kinsella and took a slip of paper from the pocket of her tunic.

"Here's a dispatch for you," she said. "God! I'm near dead! I've been on my bicycle carrying messages, without a minute's rest, since Saturday evening."

"What else do you know?" an insurgent asked her.

"The whole center of the city is in our hands," she said, "except Dublin Castle, Trinity College, the telephone exchange and a few military barracks. We'd have it all, if we

85

hadn't been betrayed. Less than a thousand turned out here in Dublin, on account of the split in the General Staff. If we'd started the fight yesterday, same as was intended, we'd have three times that many and the whole city would be ours by now. However, the enemy is hard up, too. Nearly all his officers have gone to the races at Fairyhouse."

"What's the news from our lads in the country?" said another insurgent. "Did they rise?"

"There's no news yet from the country," she said, as she moved away hurriedly towards Lower O'Connell Street. "The enemy has the telephone exchange, and the devils that were on duty in the General Post Office had put the machines in the telegraph room out of order before we managed to . . ."

Her retreating voice was drowned by the roar of the mob which had now begun to sing "God Save Ireland."

"Come on, lads," said Kinsella. "Get that barricade finished quickly. We have received further orders."

Excited by the news of victory, they completed their task in a few minutes. Then a small group of pillagers, going laden towards the west, stood on the northern pavement for a few moments, staring in anger at the wall that blocked their passage. One of them tried to climb over the barricade with a sack of flour.

"Keep back," the insurgents called out merrily. "About turn now."

The pillagers then meekly obeyed and began to force a passage towards the east through the dense crowd.

"About turn," they shouted at those in front of them.

Those nearest turned about and kept pushing those in front of them, until all of the great horde had turned and gone marching slowly towards the east, singing "God Save

Ireland." The whole channel of the street now seemed paved with human heads, above which boxes and pieces of furniture and bales of cloth and sacks of victuals swerved hither and thither, like jetsam floating along the surface of a sluggish river. Still singing, the head of the throng turned into a side street that led north to the Procathedral. The main body wound slowly after it, like a giant reptile.

Mrs. Colgan arrived as the crowd departed, with a six-quart can of tea in her hand and a large bundle of sandwiches in her apron. She was accompanied by a barefooted girl, who carried a white sack over her shoulder.

"Come on, lads," the little woman shouted. "Drink this tea before it gets cold. That's a lovely wall ye made, God bless ye. I brought ye fine beef sandwiches as well."

They gathered round her and began to tell her about the victory.

"Thanks be to God," she said, crossing herself. "Ah! God is with us, sure enough. Why wouldn't He be? Aren't we His own people?"

Then she began to spread her victuals on top of a crate that formed part of the barricade.

"It's little credit I deserve for this fine food," she chattered. "I got it all from fine neighbors. Mick Slattery gave me the beef. Poor man! He has a heart of gold. He'd be out here with his gun only for the dropsy. Teresa Daly, a poor woman that has a long family and can ill afford to be generous, gave me the tea. Ah! There's many a brave and loyal person still left in old Ireland. Teresa sent along one of her little girls with the mugs. Come on now, lads. Have at it."

Kinsella took Madden aside and said in a low voice: "Are you sure that you want to join us?"

87

Standing stiffly erect with his heels together, Madden stared into his captain's eyes like a devout person gazing at a sacred image.

"Yes, sir," he said.

Kinsella leaned against the barricade and looked at the ground.

"You didn't tell me why you want to join in the fight," he said.

A great flood of words surged into Madden's throat, trying to find an outlet. Yet he did not know how to begin speaking.

"Was it just for the sake of fighting?" Kinsella continued.

"Oh! No, sir," said Madden. "It was . . ."

He wanted to tell Kinsella about the Idea that had entered his mind while listening to the poet's voice, but he felt ashamed of doing so. In any case, the Idea was beyond his comprehension and he could not describe it, no matter how hard he tried.

"It's like this, sir," he added at length, scratching his head under the peak of his cap. "I'm not an educated man, but I'm true to my people and to the earth that bore me. I know why I want to join in this fight, but how to tell you about it is another thing."

Then he threw back his head and cried fiercely:

"All I know is that I'm ready to do your bidding, come what may."

"Are your father and mother alive?" said Kinsella.

"No, sir," Madden said. "They are both dead, Lord have mercy on them. They got the fever when I was ten years old. My sister and my two younger brothers died of it, too. They were all taken at the same time. I was the only one of the whole family that escaped. I was brought up

88

by my Uncle Patch. You might say he's all I have left in the world. A man can't count on distant relations."

"Are you married?" said Kinsella.

"No, then," said Madden, "but I was thinking of it."

He then told the story of the match he had planned and the loss of the money he had earned in England.

"So you have a girl waiting for you," said Kinsella.

"Well! Now, sir," said Madden, with a puzzled look in his eyes, "it would be hard for me to say. I hardly ever spoke to her, except to bid her the time of day."

"I see," said Kinsella. "I wanted to know whether you are free to do what you please with your life. That's why I asked you all those questions. It seems that you are."

Then he raised his head and looked at Madden.

"Before you come with me," he continued, "I must tell you that we haven't got one chance in a million of winning. All of us knew that this morning before we came out. Does that make any difference to you?"

"None at all, sir," Madden said.

"You will probably lose your life," said Kinsella, "if you come with me."

"If it's God's will that I'm to die," Madden said, "let it be so.'"

Kinsella smiled and stretched out his hand as he said: "All right, comrade."

Madden's bronzed face flushed with joy as he grasped his captain's hand.

"Thank you, sir," he said, "for letting me come with you. It's the only thing in God's world that I want."

The singing mob debouched into Upper O'Connell Street, after having gone west past the cathedral. Like flood water pouring through a broken dam, it surged out

89

into the thoroughfare, sending spearheads this way and
that among the revelers, who took up the mournful song:

> *God Save Ireland, said the heroes.*
> *God Save Ireland, said they all.*
> *Whether on the scaffold high,*
> *Or the battlefield we die,*
> *Oh! No matter when for Erin dear we fall!*

9

꟱ꟳꟲꟳꟲꟳꟲꟳꟲꟳꟲꟳꟲꟳꟲꟳꟲꟳꟲꟳ

KINSELLA recalled the two men that he had posted on lookout farther up the street. When the whole group had finished eating, he picked four of them to remain on guard at the barricade. He told the other seven that they were to come with him south of the river. Madden and Tommy Colgan were among the seven.

Mrs. Colgan was not in the least perturbed by her son's departure, although she understood that she was now finally losing contact with him for the duration of the fight. On the contrary, she was in great spirits as she bid him good-by. Madden's presence as his "miraculous protector" convinced her that Tommy would come back to her safe and sound. Furthermore, the news she had heard from the insurgents, about the battle at the South Dublin Union, had infected her with a foolish certainty of speedy victory. Indeed, it is probably unjust to call her optimism foolish. Faith has a great advantage over reason as a criterion of life's phenomena, in that it grants the believer precious moments of otherwise unattainable happiness, during the interval of waiting for the dice of fate to be cast.

"Now show your boss the stuff that's in you," she said proudly to the lad, as she brushed a crumb of bread from his tunic. "Be obedient to him and to Bartly. Have no fear, darling. The Mother of God will keep you from all harm."

It was her son who now showed emotion. He was beginning to learn that he was unable to cope with the dangerous adventure on which he had embarked with such fanatical enthusiasm. His delicate frame was not sufficiently rich in energy to meet the extravagant demands being made upon it. He clung to her as she kissed him.

"Good-by, Mother," he said almost inaudibly.

Madden also showed emotion, although of an entirely different sort. As a result of his conversation with Kinsella, he was in a state of exalted happiness. He put his arms about Mrs. Colgan's shoulders and almost crushed her frail bones in a powerful hug, in order to express his thanks for having found Kinsella through her agency.

"Have no fear, good woman," he said. "I'll keep an eye on him for you. One good turn deserves another."

She kissed his hand and cried out:

"The blessing of God on you, Bartly. May He ordain in His divine mercy to let you come back safe, together with my little son, both of you alive and kicking. Oh! May the Blessed Virgin spread her cloak over the two of you and ward off all harm."

As he marched away behind his captain southwards to the river, Madden was as much possessed by unreasoning faith as Mrs. Colgan herself. His strong and resolute young heart, however, was not concerned with mystical speculation about the receipt of help from a supernatural power. His faith was placed not in God but in Kinsella, upon whom he had seized as a symbol and embodiment of all the strange raptures that had ebbed and flowed through

92

his being since noon. These raptures had now been made constant and unchangeable by his act of faith. The Idea had become a component part of his living substance. He had been liberated from his torments by a complete surrender of himself to the authority of a leader. He no longer regretted the loss of his money, or felt any concern for his future. The farm of land and the "girl that went with it" had vanished from his mind, thrust out as irrelevant by his unique passion. He no longer had to think. That was now the affair of the somber pale-faced man with the mysterious eyes of a monk, who marched with such dignity in front of him. Like a hunting dog straining at its leash, with the scent of prey in its nostrils, his whole body was tremulous with desire to use this rifle, which could "kill the strongest beast that ever walked." His legs kept wanting to break into a run southwards, to the unknown place where he was to join in battle with an unknown enemy.

Now and again he clutched the shoulder of Tommy Colgan, who marched beside him.

"Have no fear, lad," he growled in a boastful tone. "I'm with you now, so you need have no fear. The man that touches us will meet more than his match. I'm telling you no lie."

They crossed the river without incident and turned to the left along the quays. There was nobody in sight. Only the fading tumult of the mob to the north bore evidence to the fact that the city was not at peace. When they turned to the south again, however, into a narrow street that was lined with warehouses, they suddenly came under fire. A shower of bullets from a building on the north bank of the river passed whistling over their heads.

"Get down, lads," Kinsella ordered.

Instead of obeying the command, two men fled head-long down the middle of the street. One of them dropped his rifle after he had gone a few yards. The other man squealed like a rabbit as he fled, with his cap in one hand and his rifle in the other.

"Halt!" Kinsella called after them.

Still paying no heed to their commander, the two fugitives kept running at full speed. Then they passed from sight into a lane that led to the right.

"God's curse on that pair of cowardly bastards," one of the crouching men said bitterly.

"Never mind," said Kinsella calmly. "They are a good riddance. Cowards like them would only be a handicap to us later."

Lying flat on his belly close to the brick wall of a tall warehouse, Madden swayed in the balance for a few moments between rage and the terror that had put the other two men to flight. One of the bullets had pierced his cap and passed through the hair on the right side of his skull. Then he put his hand to his cap and probed the two little holes with slow-moving fingers. As he did so, his skin began to smart slightly where the bullet had passed. Rage at once assumed mastery over terror. He cursed as he looked back over his shoulder towards the building whence the bullets had come. The firing had now ceased. The building looked dim and silent and inoffensive.

"Blood'n'ounds!" he growled. "If I could only lay my hands on the bastard that fired that shot . . ."

He ground his teeth in impotent rage against this form of combat that had been hitherto unknown to him; like a bull that issues from his dark pen and clears the arena of the little men with red cloaks in his first wild rush

94

around the barrier and then stands pawing the ground as he finds himself alone upon the sand in the blinding light and bellows in outraged majesty at the vast crowd of people that jeer at him from the stands, beyond reach of his mighty horns.

He leaned forward and gripped Tommy Colgan, who was sprawling on the pavement in front of him. The lad was trembling like a leaf.

"Are you all right, Tommy?" he whispered.

At that moment, Kinsella ordered them to move forward. Without answering Madden's question, Tommy leaped to his feet like a hare breaking cover. Then he crouched like the others and advanced slowly.

"That bastard nearly killed me," Madden growled as he followed. "I never laid eyes on him and yet he nearly killed me. What kind of bloody fighting is this?"

Without further mishap, the six remaining men reached their destination, a large red-brick building of three stories that faced a canal bridge on the main road leading south from Dublin to Dun Laoghaire. The house was already occupied by three insurgents, who removed a barricade from the hall door and admitted Kinsella's group.

"It's about time somebody came," grumbled the man in charge, as the barricade was being replaced. "We've been here since one o'clock yesterday without a word of news. I sent out two men but neither of them ever came back."

He was a student at the Veterinary College called Connie Lawless, and twenty-two years of age. His face looked much older than that, in the flickering dim light of a lantern that he held up in his left hand, to facilitate the work of his two comrades replacing the barricade. It was a crude and powerful face, with heavy jaws, thick lips and a broad nose that had been knocked out of shape in the boxing ring. The bone of his lower forehead stood out prominently above his dark eyebrows, as if a thick cord were stretched taut beneath the skin. His small deep-set blue eyes were like points of bright flame. His black hair curled straight across his forehead. He had powerfully developed shoulders and thighs. His hard muscles bulged beneath his brown turtle-neck sweater and his tight-fitting riding breeches. He wore black hobnailed top boots. There was an automatic pistol in a holster at his belt.

Madden stared in open-mouthed admiration at the enormous student.

"Blood'n'ounds!" he said to himself. "This lad is no relation at all to the mangy lot of men that I've seen until now. He'd take the sway in any crowd."

Kinsella tapped Lawless on the shoulder and said:

"Never mind. You and your comrades can have a rest now. I've been sent to take charge here."

"Blast it!" Lawless said. "We need a rest, the three of us, after being on our feet since we arrived. The civilians around here, a number of them retired army officers and well armed, have been threatening to rush us all afternoon. They would have done it, too, only for their women who kept holding them back. We felt like rats in a trap. How are things going in the city?"

Like excited children, two of the newcomers began to shout the news of insurgent successes, enlarging their extent with abandon.

"Enough of that," said Kinsella, cutting short their prattle. "Let's have a look at this place, Lawless."

In spite of his great weight, Lawless moved with extraordinary litheness. His hobnailed boots hardly made a sound as he went upstairs picking his steps daintily like a big cat.

"It's an awful kettle of fish," he said. "My company was trained specially to occupy this position, against enemy reinforcements marching on Dublin from Dun Laoghaire. Only five turned out, though, from a roll call of more than fifty. None of the officers came. I'm only a section commander. My job was to occupy an enfilading position beyond the bridge. I'll show it to you. I felt lost when I had to take command of the main position with only four men. When two of the four did a bunk later, I lost my head altogether."

"We're all in the same boat," said Kinsella, as they reached the drawing room on the second floor. "My company was trained to occupy a railway station, but I was sent instead to a useless building in the northern suburbs. Only twelve men out of eighty-six came with me. Seven of them had run away before I was recalled to headquarters and given another job. Now I have only two of my original company among the five men that I brought here."

They went to one of the drawing room windows and looked out. A small humpbacked bridge lay about fifteen yards away, spanning the still dark water of a canal. A broad avenue, brightly lit by two rows of street lamps, stretched due south from the bridge. It curved gently to the left at the far end, three hundred and fifty yards away. Four tram lines, that ran through its center, glistened faintly in the lamplight. A row of trees, widely spaced, grew by the edge of each pavement. The gentle breeze that whispered through their branches was the only sound to be heard.

Another street, that ran due east and west, cut the avenue about one hundred yards from the curve.

"That's the position I was to occupy," said Lawless, as he pointed out the house, at the near corner of the street running to the west. "Now that you're here, I had better go down there."

"I'll talk to you about that later," said Kinsella.

After examining the whole house, he posted a lookout and made the others fetch mattresses and blankets from the bedrooms into the drawing room.

"Lie down now," he told them, "and have a sleep. No talking. We have a lot of work to do, fortifying this place, as soon as it's dawn. Come with me, Lawless."

Exhausted by the events of the day, five of the men fell sound asleep almost as soon as Kinsella had left the room. Madden alone lay wide-awake, stretched out on a mattress beside Tommy Colgan, who kept trembling like a leaf struck by intermittent gusts of wind. The Connemara man lay on his back, looking out the window at the sky, which was crowded with stars. His rifle was tucked in close to his right side. He held his cap with both hands in front of his chest and he kept touching the little holes with slow-moving fingers. His whole body was rigid. It seemed to him that there was a little hammer beating against his forehead.

He felt an intense desire to kill, as he fingered the little holes. Oddly enough, it was not the man that had fired at him whom he wanted to kill. He brooded, instead, over a fight with sticks in which he and some others from his village had become engaged six years previously, on the fair green of Galway, against a crowd of men from Castlegar. The police came with drawn batons to quell the brawl. He received a blow on the right forearm that made him drop his stick. He grappled with the policeman who had struck him, only to be overwhelmed and brutally clubbed and dragged off a prisoner to the barracks. Later that evening, they came at him in his cell and kicked him until he lost consciousness. He was taken before a magistrate and given one month's hard labor. When he returned to his village, he wanted to kill whenever he met a policeman from the local garrison. Yet he did nothing, because his hands were empty and the police were armed. Now it was different. He had a weapon, a beautiful soldier's rifle that was "straight from the factory." It was the desire to use it at once, against all that had ever injured or insulted him with impunity, that caused the little hammer to keep beating time rhythmically in his head.

Some time later, Kinsella came into the room with the lantern and whispered to him:

"You all right, Madden?"

Roused from his dark brooding suddenly, his fierce eyes looked startled; just as if he had been caught by his leader doing something improper.

"Yes, sir," he mumbled.

"Go to sleep," said Kinsella. "You won't be able to do your proper share of work unless you rest."

"All right, sir," Madden said.

He turned over onto his side and closed his eyes in obedience to his captain. After Kinsella had left the room, however, he again lay on his back, looked out the window at the sky and continued his brooding. The hammer again began to strike rhythmically against the wall of his forehead. There was also a dull pain at the pit of his stomach.

He now searched through his whole life, seeking for scores that had been left unpaid. His eyes had the same fixed expression of dark rapture that he had seen in the eyes of the insurgents as they turned towards him at the portico, about to charge the General Post Office.

10

Jーㄩーㄩーㄩーㄩーㄩーㄩーㄩーㄩーㄩーㄩーㄩーㄩーㄩーㄩ

N<small>EXT</small> <small>MORNING</small> after breakfast, Kinsella addressed the little garrison in the drawing room. He was a science professor at a secondary school in the city. He spoke in a calm and detached manner, as if he were explaining some problem to his students in the seclusion of his laboratory. His pale refined features showed no emotion.

"Courageous men," he said, "fight best when they have no illusions. So I'm telling you quite frankly that our position is desperate. It is true that we have captured some important positions in the city, but we are unable to exploit our initial advantage. Less than a thousand of our men turned out and hardly more than a fourth of our officers. For the moment, the enemy is unable to dislodge us, having stripped Ireland of combat troops to feed his armies in France. He must get reinforcements from England before attempting to crush us. When those troops arrive, only a miracle can save us. That miracle is help from our comrades in the provinces. Unless they take up arms, in spite of the countermanding order sent out last Saturday by our Chief of Staff, we are doomed. If we hold out long enough, they may rise. All told, we have nearly twenty thousand men scattered throughout Ireland.

Human nature being what it is, the great majority of them were probably glad to receive the countermanding order, after the capture last Friday of the ship bringing us arms from abroad. When they find out, however, that Dublin has risen in spite of all and is holding out, they may be spurred into action to save their honor. Our job, comrades, is to give them that chance by holding the bridge out in front here, against those enemy reinforcements coming from England. We must hold it to the last man, or the last round of ammunition. We must hang on desperately to the last moment; because every moment that we resist in arms makes certain that our sacrifice will bear fruit in making our comrades in the provinces and our whole people begin to fight. Even if we are crushed and lose our lives, our rising will still be victorious, if we set an example of courage to the people of Ireland, an example that will make them take up arms and fight for their freedom. Come on now, lads. Get to work and prepare to defend this bridge."

The hammer was still beating against Madden's forehead while Kinsella spoke. He still felt a dull pain at the pit of his stomach and his whole body was unpleasantly taut. Yet he experienced intense happiness as he listened to the voice and watched the face of the man he now worshiped with religious fanaticism. He had once felt an intense happiness of that sort as a boy, on seeing a look of ecstasy in the eyes of an old priest he was serving at Mass. His hand had then trembled so violently that his little goblet rattled against the rim of the chalice as he poured the wine.

All the other men, except Tommy Colgan, who sulked in the background with downcast head, were roused to a great pitch of enthusiasm by what their commander had said. They cared nothing at the moment about the gravity of their position. They were spoiling for a fight and indifferent to its outcome.

They began to fortify the drawing room. It was very large and exposed. The front wall consisted of three large windows that stretched nearly the whole way from floor to ceiling, with narrow piers of brickwork intervening. In order to provide cover before the windows, they tore all the available blankets into strips, which they sewed into bags and stuffed with earth from the back garden.

As they began to place these improvised bags in position before the window to the right, one of the men so engaged saw a horse and cab go slowly past the house towards the bridge. He was a bricklayer called Nicholas Holden, a tall fair-haired fellow with a freckled face, wearing a green-colored set of equipment over his blue serge suit.

"Hey! Louis," he called out to the jarvey, "were you at the races?"

The jarvey halted his horse, gathered a number of ragged overcoats closer about his thin body, hiccoughed and looked up at the window. He had only one eye.

"Who's that?" he said with a drunken lisp. "Who spoke to me?"

"Cripes! You must have a proper load on you," said Holden. "It's Nick. Don't you know your own butty?"

"Oh! Hello, Nick!" said the jarvey.

"Were you at Fairyhouse yesterday?" said Holden.

"I was there all right," said the jarvey.

He hiccoughed again and then jerked his thumb back-

103

wards in the direction of two large men, who were sound asleep in the interior of the cab, with their hats drawn down over their eyes.

"These two members," he added, "wouldn't risk coming into town last night on account of the ructions. They made me turn back to the Dead Man Murray's place, where we're after spending the night."

"What won the Irish National?" said Holden anxiously.

The jarvey belched and set his horse in motion once more.

"All Sorts won it in a canter," he said.

"All Sorts!" cried Holden in a tone of horror. "A rank outsider! Aw! By the hammers of hell!"

One of the other fellows at the window now threw up his arm in a gesture of triumph. He was a newsboy called Martin Lynch, commonly called "Skinny" owing to his thin and stunted body. He was over eighteen, but he looked no bigger than a child. His lips moved like those of a person with a stammer trying in vain to speak.

"You could get any price you liked about him," said the jarvey, as his tired nag walked slowly westwards. "Any bloody price you wanted."

"Where was Turkish Maiden?" shouted the enraged Holden.

"Never in the picture," said the jarvey.

Then he started and looked at Holden intently, with terror in his solitary eye.

"Hey, Nick," he cried, "do you mean to tell me that you are . . . ?"

He stopped speaking, looked to his front, lashed his exhausted horse into a fumbling gallop and passed from sight along the southern bank of the canal.

"All Sorts!" muttered Holden in disgust. "Cripes! I thought Turkish Maiden was a racing certainty."

The little newsboy suddenly found voice and cried out:

"My mother backed All Sorts. She got him in a dream. Honest to God, she dreamt he'd win it. She pledged damn near everything we had in the house with Dick Burgess to get the necessary. She had over a quid on him. Twenty-two and a tanner, to be exact."

He turned to Holden and added:

"What price was the winner?"

Holden struck the lad on the right ear with the back of his hand. The newsboy staggered backwards, put his hand to his ear and gaped at Holden with a hurt look in his eyes, like a dog that has been struck by its master for no good reason.

Madden entered the room as the blow was struck. He threw down two bags he was carrying and strode over to Holden.

"You had no right to do that," he said.

"What's it got to do with you?" Holden retorted. "I had a couple of bob on the favorite and then this little chiseler comes along, yapping about how his mother won on an outsider, as the result of a bloody dream. He even asked me, mind you . . . "

"Only a coward would strike a lad that's only half his size," said Madden in an offensive tone.

Holden pushed him in the chest with his clenched fist and said truculently:

"You run along and mind your own business, or you might get a . . ."

Madden floored the bricklayer with a right to the jaw.

"What's going on here?" said Kinsella, who entered the room just then.

Madden put his heels together and pointed at Holden, who had leaped to his feet at once in order to retaliate.

"Sorry, sir," he said gruffly, "but that man hit me and I had to hit back. I couldn't do anything else."

He then lowered his glance to the floor, ashamed of what he had done in the presence of his captain. The truth was that he had not been at all offended with Holden for striking the newsboy. He had deliberately picked a quarrel with the bricklayer in order to ease the tension of his nerves and make the hammer stop beating by an outburst of violence. Now the hammer had stopped as a result of his striking the blow — and he felt quite relaxed, even though he was ashamed of having annoyed Kinsella.

"I only gave the bloody fellow a shove with the back of my hands," said Holden to Kinsella indignantly, "and he let fly at me with all he had."

"Back or front," said Madden, with his eyes still downcast, "a blow is a blow and has to be answered. A man has to strike back whenever he's hit."

Then he turned to Holden, towards whom he really felt grateful for enabling him to stop the hammer.

"No bad feelings, though," he added.

"All right," said Holden, "but don't be in such a hurry next time. You're not the only man that can . . ."

"That's enough, Holden," said Kinsella. "Get on with your work."

Then he turned towards Madden and added severely:

"There must be no more of this childishness. You're now a soldier and you must learn to behave like one. You

106

are to fight the enemy and not your comrades. It's not your business to maintain order here, or to correct injustice. I'm in command. You understand?"

"Yes, sir," Madden said respectfully.

Instead of being hurt by Kinsella's reprimand, he felt delighted at being punished at once for his misbehavior. In fact, he felt that the hard words established a bond of comradeship between himself and his captain.

"There's a man for you," he said to himself as he rushed back to work with enthusiasm. "To look at him, you'd think butter wouldn't melt in his mouth, but he's as hard as iron. Ah! Lord God! That man has the stuff in him all right!"

To east and west and north, there was now sporadic firing of rifles and machine guns and the crash of exploding bombs. Just as a ballet dancer struts about behind the scenes on tiptoe and leaps into the air to test his muscles, on hearing the confused tumult of the orchestra being tuned before the curtain's rise, Madden felt these distant sounds of battle acting as a goad, urging him to hasten preparations for the dance of death in which he was going to take part.

All through the morning, there was no interference by the civilians of the neighborhood. Men and women came from the three-storied red-brick houses that lined the avenue, with shopping baskets on their arms. They glanced furtively at the breastworks growing in the drawing-room windows, as they hurried across the bridge to purchase food; and again when they returned to their homes with their baskets laden. Some stood in their doorways for a few moments and stared northwards at the outpost. A few daring ones strolled about the little gardens

107

that fronted their houses, affecting an indifference that was false. They were all silent and apprehensive, like birds that sense the approach of an unseen hawk.

Towards noon, however, when the breastworks were finished and the insurgents were stripping the drawing room of its furniture, an old man came from a house that lay about seventy yards south of the bridge. He was wearing the full-dress uniform of an infantry colonel. His greatcoat was unbuttoned. He carried a revolver in his right hand and in his left a walking stick, on which he leaned heavily. Holding himself erect with extreme difficulty, he came towards the bridge at a slow uncertain pace, stumbling at intervals like a person just recovered from a severe illness. An old woman equally decrepit came after him, gesticulating with her left hand and holding up her skirt with her right. She kept calling out his name in a high-pitched tremulous voice. She caught up with him when he had almost reached the bridge and took him by the left shoulder. He halted, stared at the outpost, brandished his revolver and cried out: "As an Irishman and a loyal subject of His Majesty . . ." Then he collapsed and allowed himself to be led away by the old woman, who cried out in a plaintive tone: "Oh, Hector, how could you do such a thing?" Two other women came and helped her take him home. They practically had to carry the old fellow, who had now fallen into a semiconscious state as a result of his physical effort and the passion that inflamed his soul.

After removing the furniture and the window hangings, the insurgents drew up the mattresses before the breastworks, to make the firing positions more comfortable. They stored their rations, medical supplies and reserve

108

ammunition on the landing, together with some pails of water for use in case of fire.

Then Kinsella took Lawless aside and said:

"How many men do you want to take with you to the advance post?"

"Just Coleman Walsh," Lawless said.

He called Walsh, who approached lazily with the rolling gait of a seaman. Walsh was forty-three years old and even larger than Lawless himself. A heavy blue woolen jersey covered his enormous barrel-shaped torso, with the words "Mary-Ellen" painted in white across his chest. His smooth full face was tanned dark brown. There was a constant expression of amazement in his shining black eyes. His oval-shaped head was planted slantwise on his thick short neck, like a Rugby football balanced for a place kick. An automatic pistol lay in a holster at his belt. He nodded to Kinsella and then stood leaning forward from his hips, with his hands clasped under the back of his unbuttoned blue jacket. His weight was on his left foot. His right foot was thrust far out in front of him.

Kinsella looked the big sailor up and down slowly.

"Do you think one man is enough?" he said to Lawless.

"Any more would only be in the way," Lawless said. "Automatics make short work of ammunition and we have only five hundred rounds. Even for two men, that's no great shakes."

Walsh kept nodding his head gravely as Lawless spoke.

"All right," said Kinsella. "Let it be just the two of you."

"If you could spare us a little more stuff," said Lawless eagerly, "or a couple of revolvers, in case . . ."

"I'm afraid that's impossible," said Kinsella. "We are very short of ammunition and we need the three revolvers that we have, for close-quarter firing."

Lawless shrugged his shoulders.

"Don't you think it's time for us to be going down there now?" he said.

"Not yet," said Kinsella. "They promised to send me word when the enemy is approaching. You must wait until the last moment, for fear some scout might discover your presence there and have time to pass along a warning. Surprise is everything in an ambush."

Then he turned towards the others and said:

"Empty your ammunition pouches."

Lawless and Walsh went to a corner and sat down on the floor with their backs to the rear wall. They began to whisper with their heads close together; like two gladiators waiting to enter the arena for a bout, already detached from their fellows and from life.

"All told," said Kinsella, after he had counted the ammunition that had been dumped onto a mattress, "we have only about two thousand rounds of rifle ammunition. I needn't tell you, lads, that it's very little and that you must be very careful with every single round."

A red-haired shop assistant called Jeremiah Murphy took off his cap, threw it on the floor and cursed:

"Isn't that the bloody limit?" he said. "There's nearly twenty thousand rounds in the cellar of the house where I lodge. There's a lot of gelignite there as well. The lad that was supposed to come and fetch it in a taxi never came. When I went to his place, his mother told me that he had gone to the races with a party. The races!"

Kinsella divided the ammunition into three parts, which

110

he placed on strips of blanket by the windows, in a handy position for reloading quickly under fire. Then he assigned the men their windows. Madden and Tommy Colgan were given the window to the left. Holden and a man called Paddy Furlong took the one on the right. He himself took the deserter's rifle to the big bay window in the center, together with Murphy. He put Lynch in reserve, to fetch food and supplies and to douse fires with water from the pails.

After another meal, they rehearsed the battle tactics that Kinsella had devised until nightfall. Then they lay down on their mattresses before the breastworks.

"What's the matter, lad?" Madden whispered to Tommy Colgan, when they were stretched out together at their window. "Don't you feel well?"

Tommy had been sulking all day, doing hardly any work and resisting the occasional efforts that Madden made to establish friendly contact with him. He now lay on his belly, with his face thrust down behind his crossed arms. He did not reply.

"Why the hell don't you speak?" Madden continued.

As he still received no answer, he thumped the lad in the side and growled:

"What sort of a fellow are you? Blood'n'ounds! You are a fine comrade to have fighting alongside me!"

Tommy drew away a little and said in a pettish tone without raising his head:

"Leave me alone. I just want to be left alone."

"All right, then," said Madden. "Have it your own way."

He did not insist any further. In spite of his promise to Mrs. Colgan, his "unique passion" now left very little room in his mind for concern about Tommy's welfare. He

111

had completely forgotten the lad a few moments later, as he fingered his cartridge clips and his rifle and peered over the parapet at the avenue, along which the unknown enemy would soon come marching.

He felt deliriously excited. It was the same sort of excitement, only much more intense, that he had felt one night when he was sixteen, while going after wild duck with a stonemason who had a muzzle-loading shotgun. They had lain in the reeds by the edge of a lake for two hours before the ducks came.

He no longer felt any tension or pain. The hammer had stopped beating. He was not even aware of a desire to kill.

11

A MAN APPROACHED the outpost at dawn and said on being challenged that he had come with a message from headquarters. Kinsella ran downstairs to meet him.

"Hello, Michael!" he said on being admitted. "I was told to warn you that several thousand enemy troops have landed at Dun Laoghaire and are now marching on Dublin."

He was George Stapleton, a delicately built man of twenty-six, with prominent cheekbones, brilliant blue eyes and a broad overarching forehead. There was no trace of color in his hollow cheeks. He wore a Volunteer uniform, but he carried no weapon or equipment of any sort. The uniform hung loosely about his emaciated frame, as if he were a child masquerading in the clothes of a grown-up person. He was of middle height, but he looked very short at the moment, being bent almost double under the weight of a big sack that was slung from his left shoulder. His burden made his face look terribly strained and there were beads of sweat standing out on his forehead. Yet he was smiling broadly, like a man enjoying himself thoroughly. His teeth were beautifully white and regular.

Kinsella shook hands warmly with the newcomer. They had been close friends for the past two years.

113

"I'm so glad you've come, George," said Kinsella. "Do you know when they set out? Are they near here?"

"I've no idea," said Stapleton, gasping for breath. "I got the message two hours ago. It has taken me all that time to come, owing to a patrol I met. I had to hide . . ."

"In that case," said Kinsella, as he turned towards the stairs, "there is no time to waste."

As Stapleton followed, bending low under his sack, he began to talk at breakneck speed. In spite of his manifest exhaustion, he still smiled radiantly and his eyes sparkled.

"How good this is!" he cried. "I know that I'm terribly late and that I should have rushed into action at once, when the man came to mobilize me on Monday morning. I really was not as ill as I pretended to be. It was merely a nervous headache. Indeed, I now confess quite frankly that I didn't come with him because I was afraid; not of dying but of proving to be a coward. Oh yes, I was awfully afraid of discovering that I might be unable to behave properly under fire! All my life, as I have often told you, I had been trying to prepare myself for that moment of heroism and yet, when it came, I found that I had . . ."

He stopped speaking and halted, with his left foot on the second step of the stairway, on noticing that Kinsella had passed from sight. Then he sighed wearily, gripped the banisters and continued to mount with great difficulty. His legs swayed from side to side like those of a drunken person.

"He's coming, lads," Kinsella cried as he came into the drawing room at a run. "Get ready for action, all of you. Remove the windowpanes. Lynch, go and get tea ready."

With the exception of Tommy Colgan, the men were

114

already on their feet, waiting anxiously for the news brought by the messenger. They rushed at once to obey. Tommy Colgan remained lying face downwards on his mattress, with his arms crossed before his forehead. He showed no sign of having heard Kinsella's command. Yet he was wide-awake and listening intently to what was happening.

"Now is your time," Kinsella said to Lawless and Walsh. "Get your kit and be on your way."

"We're ready," Lawless said. "Come on, Coleman."

They picked up two small sacks from the corner where they had spent the night.

"Have you got everything clear in your minds?" Kinsella asked them.

They both nodded.

"Are you quite sure?" said Kinsella.

"Don't worry," said Lawless. "There won't be any slip."

"All right, lads," said Kinsella. "Good luck to you."

The two men stalked out of the room as Stapleton entered.

"Hey! You!" cried Kinsella, as he rushed across to Tommy Colgan. "What are you doing there?"

The lad did not reply or make any move. Kinsella had to turn him over on his back before he looked up sideways at his commander, holding his bent left arm before his face, as if expecting a blow. There was stark terror in his eyes.

"I'm sick at the stomach," he muttered.

Kinsella knew at once what troubled the lad. He glanced over his shoulder at Stapleton.

"Are you staying with us, George?" he said.

Stapleton was now sitting in the middle of the floor

with his legs stretched out, fanning his face with his uniform cap. His fair hair needed cutting badly.

"Of course," he said. "I've no rifle — but I have a revolver and quite a lot of ammunition. . . . Couldn't find my rifle anywhere. You know what my aunt's house is like."

"You have a revolver and ammunition?" said Kinsella. Stapleton pointed to the sack and said:

"They are in there. My aunt . . ."

"Let me have them," said Kinsella as he hurried across the floor. "I want to give them to . . ."

He opened the mouth of the sack and dumped its contents on the floor. It disgorged a varied collection of foodstuffs, in addition to a revolver and a box of ammunition. There were four large loaves of Hovis bread, ten packets of Jacob's biscuits, a dozen tins of preserved meat and fruit, a ham, a cheese, two pounds of butter, a pound of tea, a pound of sugar, a score of hard-boiled eggs and a bottle of brandy.

"My aunt insisted on my taking all these things," said Stapleton, as Kinsella ran back to Madden's window with the revolver and the box of ammunition. "She does the most absurd things at times. I'm sure she gave away my rifle to some poor person by mistake, in a box of old clothes. 'My dear boy,' she said, when I objected to taking the hamper, 'my late husband was a soldier and he loved only two things in life, eating and killing. Soldiers are all alike. They're horrid people.' It was no use arguing with her. Good Lord! You have no idea how heavy these things have been. I felt tempted to throw away the wretched sack and yet . . ."

After breaking all the panes of glass in his window,

116

Madden came over to Tommy Colgan and shook him roughly.

"Get up out of that," he said, "and don't bring shame on your mother."

"Leave him alone, Madden," said Kinsella, who was looking out the window, waiting for Lawless and Walsh to emerge from the hall door. "I have told you already not to interfere with your comrades."

"I'm sorry, sir," said Madden, "but I promised his mother that I'd keep an eye on him for her."

Lawless and Walsh came out of the house at that moment.

Kinsella called down to them.

"Catch," he said.

He threw down the revolver and the box of ammunition, which they caught neatly.

"Thanks," Lawless said as they moved towards the bridge.

"Stand by, lads," said Kinsella, "for fear they might be attacked on the way over."

Lawless and Walsh marched southwards at a sauntering pace along the western side of the avenue, after crossing the bridge. There was nobody else in sight. All was still. The leaves of the trees looked quite black in the dim light of dawn. Walsh rolled along with his head thrust forward and his arms dangling limply from his sloping shoulders. The sack in his left hand looked tiny in comparison with his enormous body.

Lawless now carried a rolled overcoat slung across his back. He moved with the perfect rhythm of a trained athlete, picking his steps daintily. When they came abreast of the house they were to occupy, they suddenly vaulted

117

over the iron railing that fronted the garden and then ran headlong to a basement window, which they smashed with their boots. A little later, the hall door opened slightly and an outstretched hand was waved for a moment.

"Go downstairs," Kinsella told Tommy Colgan, who was now sitting on the edge of his mattress, staring fixedly at the floor, "and send up Murphy, who is on guard down there. Your job will be to watch the back entrance and give Lynch a hand."

The lad picked up his rifle and jumped to his feet with a sudden access of energy, being roused from his apathy by the prospect of escape from view of the dread avenue along which the soldiers would soon come marching.

"Leave your rifle," said Kinsella.

Tommy halted in his tracks and glanced at his rifle. He was loath to part with the weapon, which he had purchased out of his meager wages, by subscribing a few pence each week. Then he put it down on the mattress and left the room, dragging his feet after him. He sobbed convulsively on reaching the landing. Then he straightened himself and rushed headlong downstairs.

"You'll take Colgan's place, George," Kinsella said to Stapleton. "It's a great stroke of luck for us to get a crack shot like you at the last moment. It's a good omen."

Stapleton got to his feet, came over to Madden's window and picked up Tommy's rifle.

"Blood'n'ounds!" Madden said to himself, as he looked with hostility at the strange fellow that was now to be his fighting companion. "What sort of a galoot is this? The other lad turned out to be a coward, but he looked like a king compared to this one."

118

Stapleton examined the rifle and said:

"Seems all right, but I really prefer to use a revolver. It's more intimate somehow."

Madden scratched his head as he continued to watch the extraordinary man, who had the face and manners and speech of "a grand gentleman" and yet behaved like a garrulous empty-headed woman. Added to that, the fellow was dressed like a scarecrow. He puzzled the Connemara man, who had never before come in contact with such a person. What puzzled him most was that Stapleton examined the rifle like an expert and that his lunatic face became serious as soon as he touched the weapon.

When Lynch arrived with a big kettle of hot tea, they had an enormous breakfast. In view of the great hamper of food brought by Stapleton, Kinsella told them not to stint themselves.

"You may not get another chance to eat for some time," he said.

Then they cleaned and loaded their weapons and lay down to wait in their firing positions; all except Kinsella, who kept moving about to see that everything was in order for battle.

"I dare say," Stapleton said to Madden, as they lay side by side before their window, "that you dislike having an odd fellow like myself for a comrade. I can see that you have no confidence in me. You probably think that I'll faint or go into hysterics when the fighting starts. That remains to be seen. Even I myself don't know. That's partly why I'm here. Goodness knows, I should be excellent at this sort of thing, unless I'm a changeling. All my people have been professional soldiers for hundreds of years. My father commands a division on the Flanders front and my two brothers are on active service in the Middle East. I've been practically an invalid most of my life, so you see . . . Well! You know how small boys behave towards a chap that can't play games. They disliked me, just as you do now and for the same reason. My interest in ideas, really, may be just a form of protest against my isolation. In any case, my father wanted me to take Holy Orders, saying that I didn't seem to be good for anything else; meaning, of course, that I was unfit for military service. He cut me off when I refused to become a parson. I've been living with my Aunt Mary ever since. She too is an outcast, more or less, since she ran away from her husband with an English painter. She's a marvelously civilized person, having associated for years on the Continent with the most brilliant people of her day in art and letters. Since her return to Ireland, she has kept open house at Foxrock for people with advanced ideas. That was how I met Michael. Not that revolution interests me, really, except as a spectator. I love only poetry and music, to be quite candid with you. At the same time, any form of beauty, in which I include war, at least in the sense that it is a supreme expression of human passion . . ."

Madden paid absolutely no heed to what the garrulous fellow was saying. He had passed into a strange state, in which he himself had ceased to exist as a separate entity, now that the wild ducks were approaching on the wing.

He had become united in spirit with the unknown enemy and his body had no other function than to wait, without conscious feeling, for the moment of contact.

12

⊓⊔⊓⊔⊓⊔⊓⊔⊓⊔⊓⊔⊓⊔⊓⊔⊓⊔⊓⊔⊓⊔⊓⊔⊓⊔⊓

IT WAS ALMOST NOON when Paddy Furlong
called out suddenly:

"He's coming!"

They all examined the avenue excitedly in response to
his cry; but they could neither see nor hear anything sig-
nificant. Then they looked at Furlong, who was listening
intently with his head turned to one side and his forehead wrinkled vertically between his eyes.

"What do you hear, Paddy?" said Kinsella.

Furlong was the tall gray-haired man in a shabby belted
raincoat whom Madden had seen march beside Tommy
Colgan across O'Connell Street on Monday night. His face
was the color of old parchment. He had drooping gray
mustaches and bushy eyebrows that were still partly
brown. A saber scar ran down his right cheek, from the
outer corner of his eye to the rear end of his jaw. He had
a big cud of tobacco in his cheek.

"I hear nothing at all," he said, in the bored voice of a
man that has seen a great deal of the world and is no
longer capable of astonishment. "I know he's coming all
the same. You'll see him any moment now."

"Why do you think so?" said Kinsella.

Furlong shrugged his shoulders and said:

121

"I couldn't tell you, Captain, but I know he's coming. I feel him."

"Arrah! For God's sake," Murphy said in his singsong voice, "that man is crazy. There are only sparrows and a black cat to be seen out there."

"Never mind," Furlong said calmly. "I was a soldier for twenty years. I've waited for the enemy scores of times, just like this, on the Northwest Frontier, in Afghanistan, in the Sudan and in South Africa. You get to have second sight from the strain of . . ."

"Ha!" cried Holden in a tense whisper. "There he is."

"Blood'n'ounds!" Madden said.

All eyes became fixed on two soldiers that had come into view three hundred and fifty yards away, at the point where the avenue curved gently towards the left.

"How beautiful this is!" Stapleton whispered.

Madden drew in a deep breath through his nostrils. As he opened his lips to exhale, he settled his body down against the mattress, slowly and almost imperceptibly, like a setter dog lapsing into immobility with infinite caution, before spotted game.

"Steady now, lads," said Kinsella. "Wait for the command to fire and remember that every round is precious. No shooting at random. Take steady aim at a target each time before you fire."

The two soldiers advanced very slowly, one on each pavement, with their rifles at the high port. Their fixed bayonets glistened in the bright sunlight. They kept glancing warily at the houses on either side of the avenue. Then one of them halted, looked to his rear and waved his arm forward twice in a half circle. A few moments later two other soldiers appeared. They were followed by several

122

other pairs, all marching in Indian file on either pavement, at intervals of about six feet, with their bayoneted rifles at the high port. The brightly polished buttons and cap badges of those in the lead were now plainly visible to the insurgents watching from the drawing room.

"Holden and Furlong will fire to the left," said Kinsella. "Murphy, Stapleton and Madden will fire to the right."

Even though he was now in sight of the imperial soldiers, whose uniforms had hitherto aroused dull hatred and resentment in him, Madden was still without conscious feeling. Indeed, through some extraordinary change that had taken place in him, he now looked upon the strange yellow creatures as parts of himself, united to him by a mysterious bond. He aimed his weapon at one of them with complete unconcern.

The main body of the imperial troops now came into view, a short distance to the rear of the leading files, marching in two parallel columns of route, with the sections of fours widely spaced, along both sides of the avenue. Their movement was like a dance. Each column halted at intervals and lay down on the pavement, until the column on the opposite side of the avenue had caught up and preceded it a short distance. The slow rhythmic tramp of their advancing feet became a confused shuffle as they threw themselves down. They were about eight hundred strong.

"Steady now, lads," said Kinsella, as the leading column came abreast of the house where the two insurgents were lying in ambush. "Wait for the word of command and don't hurry."

A sustained burst of fire came suddenly from the automatic pistols of Lawless and Walsh. Two soldiers dropped

123

their rifles, opened out their arms and then swayed forward with bowed heads, as if making a profound gesture of obeisance. Three others fell straight down together and lay still abruptly.

"Rapid fire!" said Kinsella.

The soldiers broke in disorder as bullets swept their ranks from both front and flank.

"Take cover," their officers shouted.

The two columns, that had been moving forward with disciplined precision, now became a formless mass. Dropping their rifles to the trail position in order to run faster, the soldiers stabbed one another in the rear with their bayonets and trod with indifference on the bodies of their fallen comrades. Some went into the side street that ran to the east. Others leaped over the iron railings of the little gardens that bordered the left-hand pavement. There they sprawled behind hedges and evergreen shrubs. A number of those in the extreme rear bolted pell-mell towards the south, paying no heed to the shouts of their officers, who tried to control their movements.

There was a strange silence after all the fugitives had taken cover, like the pause between two movements of a symphony. Then one of the wounded got to his feet on the roadway. He threw out his right arm towards the gardens in which his comrades had taken shelter, uttered a hoarse cry and fell on his back, with his left knee bent.

There was a scarlet patch on the right breast of his yellow tunic.

As if in answer to the cry, those in the gardens opened fire on the advance post. Then an elderly colonel of great height, elegant in fawn-colored riding breeches and shin-

124

ing brown top boots, jumped to his feet and made a circle with his naked sword above his head.

"Charge!" he shouted.

As he plunged through an open gateway onto the pavement, two other officers jumped to their feet and drew their swords.

"Charge!" they shouted.

About fifty other ranks followed the three officers into the roadway, with their bayonets leveled.

"Hurrah! Hurrah! Hurrah!" they shouted.

The elderly colonel fell when he was halfway across the roadway. One of the other two officers fell almost immediately afterwards. The last reached the edge of the pavement before he fell.

The men then broke and fled to cover, leaving behind eight of their number.

Murphy uttered a shout of triumph after the order to cease fire.

"We're the lads for them," he cried boastfully. "I bet they're sorry they left home by now."

Kinsella told his men to reload their weapons.

"Keep your heads well down, fellows," he added. "He must have spotted us by now. He'll be heading our way presently."

Madden found great difficulty in reloading his weapon. From the moment that he had begun to fire at the soldiers, he had been carried away by an outburst of passion; as a man that holds within his grasp a long-sought mistress and strives with all his living strength to thrust the pent-up fever from his blood. He trembled so much that his hand was unable to force down the cartridges from the clip into the magazine of his rifle.

125

"Lord God!" he cried out in a voice that had again become slightly high-pitched, as he fumbled impotently. "This is a rifle fit for the greatest king that ever walked the earth. It doesn't kick or shake or move the least part of an inch when you fire it. Blood'n'ounds! The lightest touch on the trigger is enough. Sure, I never knew I was firing it at all."

Then Stapleton, who had already loaded his own weapon, turned towards the Connemara man and said:

"Let me do it for you."

He reached over and forced down the cartridges deftly, in one movement of his delicate fingers.

"The idea is to press gently and steadily," he said, "otherwise you . . ."

He stopped speaking and turned sharply to his front as the soldiers opened fire on the drawing room. Bullets spattered against the outer wall of the house and against the breastworks. A few entered the room through the open parts of the windows overhead and embedded themselves in the rear wall.

"Steady, lads," said Kinsella. "Wait until he shows himself. Don't fire until I give the order."

The soldiers continued to fire into both insurgent posts for more than five minutes. Then about seventy of them dashed from the side street that led to the east. Five of their number fell as they debouched into the avenue and turned north towards the bridge, spread out across the whole width of the thoroughfare. The two officers who led the charge were among the fallen. A large man with pointed mustaches then dashed to the front and took command. He wore the crown of a company sergeant-major on the left forearm of his tunic. The men ran bravely after

126

him to the bridge, falling one by one. At first the tramp of their hobnailed boots was loud. As their numbers thinned, however, it was drowned by the noise of gunfire. More than half of them had fallen by the time their leader reached the foot of the slope leading to the bridge. There he also fell. The rest then turned and fled, still falling one by one, leaving their fallen comrades on the roadway, like yellow sheaves of corn strewn over a shorn field behind a line of reapers.

The sergeant-major lay motionless for a few moments. Then he crawled to his rifle, which had skidded a little way on being dropped. He seized it, struggled to his feet and staggered forward, muttering obscene curses. His dropping blood made a scarlet trail behind him. A large bald spot, like a monk's tonsure, showed at the top of his unhatted skull. Two more bullets struck him, but he struggled on with extraordinary courage to the summit of the bridge. There he received his deathblow in the throat. He dropped his rifle a second time, fell over the parapet and sank to the bottom of the canal. He reappeared almost at once, opened his jaws wide like a strangled fish and sank again to rise no more.

When the firing ceased, Holden whispered to Kinsella and then ran headlong to the lavatory.

"Blood'n'ounds!" Madden said to Stapleton. "Did you see that bald fellow? There's a lad that had the stuff in him. He must have been the champion of his crowd. They're going to miss him. By Ganeys! It was a pity to have to draw the blood of a warrior like him."

"It's most extraordinary," Stapleton said in a dreamy tone. "Not in the least what I expected."

His face was now solemn and reverent, as if something

127

wonderful had just been made manifest to him; something that enlarged his consciousness of the infinite universe by which he was encompassed and which he was unable to comprehend in its entirety, because he formed part of it and could only realize its existence through the tumult of his senses.

"What's that?" Madden said.

"The emotion is almost more than I can bear," said Stapleton, "like listening to music. Yet there is an element of sensual delight . . . "

"What the hell are you talking about?" Madden interrupted.

He himself was no longer disturbed by emotion of any sort, now that he had recovered from the first passionate frenzy of contact with his partners in the dance of death. He had settled down to the business of fighting with cool determination and efficiency.

"It's quite impossible for me to explain," said Stapleton, as he looked out the window at the sky. "One can't describe things that are purely sensual. They are beyond words. Passion is silent."

Three stretcher-bearers crawled out to the wounded that lay south of the advance post. A few moments later, a woman in nurse's uniform came up to the bridge from the street that flanked the outpost to the west. As she reached the hump, she glanced over her shoulder contemptuously at an insurgent who advised her to turn back. Five other women crossed the bridge after her.

"Stretch your legs, lads," said Kinsella. "He won't do anything while those women are out there. Any tea left in the kettle, Lynch?"

The six nurses went among the wounded who lay im-

128

mediately south of the bridge. One of them carried a pail of drinking water and a cup. The others bandaged the wounds, tearing their aprons into strips when their supply of ready-made bandages was exhausted. Then they picked up three of the wounded, two to each man. As they began to carry them across the bridge, those left behind moaned piteously.

"Beautiful!" said Stapleton. "Like huge white ants dragging yellow captives to their lair."

They had just finished drinking the tea that Lynch brought when the soldiers again charged; this time without any preparatory fire. There were only thirty men in the charge. Stripped of their heavy equipment and armed only with hand grenades, they ran so fast that only three of them had fallen before they reached the bridge. Then Kinsella and three other insurgents stood up against the brickwork piers to attack them with the Mauser pistol and revolvers. The quick-firing weapons littered the hump of the bridge with fallen bodies in a few moments. The remaining soldiers fled. One of them threw a hand grenade as he turned. It did not explode. The man had forgotten to draw the pin.

The imperial troops continued to attack in this senseless way for more than three hours without improving their position. Their losses were very heavy. The gray roadway became spotted like a leopard's hide by the yellow bodies of the fallen. Green branches, torn from the trees by bullets, lay here and there upon the corpses like loving tokens of remembrance. The insurgents remained unharmed. Their ammunition, however, was beginning to run low and the strain on their nerves became acute, from being constantly pinned down to their firing positions.

129

During the intervals between attacks, Madden became increasingly irritated, as he realized the enemy was a beast that his beautiful rifle could maim but not kill. This beast was a colossus, armed with hundreds of yellow limbs, which he kept thrusting forward towards the bridge with indomitable will. Several hundred of those limbs had been severed. There they lay upon the roadway, some writhing in agony and others motionless in death. Yet many hundred more still kept coming forward to attack.

As a man bedded with an insatiable wanton, he became enraged with these yellow creatures whom he could not master, while waiting idly on his mattress after an attack had been repelled. Yet when they charged again and he began to fire his rifle at them, his rage changed into a mysterious and satisfying feeling of unity with these men, on whom he spent his passion.

13

AT FOUR O'CLOCK a large number of fresh troops arrived on the scene and went into action under more intelligent command. They planted machine guns at points of vantage and poured uninterrupted fire into both insurgent posts. They also fanned out along their left flank, enveloped the advance post and attacked it from the rear with hand grenades.

Unable to help their doomed comrades, the men in the drawing room listened to the explosion of the grenades in bitter idleness. Then they heard a cheer come from the captured house. The soldiers along the avenue joined in the cheering. Presently, two bayoneted rifles were waved from a ground floor window of the house. A man's cap was perched on the point of each bayonet.

"They're down," said Holden, crossing himself. "Lord have mercy on their souls."

Made senseless by rage, Murphy jumped to his feet and shouted:

"You bastards!"

He leveled his rifle at the window from which the caps were being waved and took aim.

"Get down," Kinsella shouted at him.

A cluster of machine-gun bullets struck the hapless man

in the face just as Kinsella reached up to seize him. The upper part of his body jerked sharply backwards. Kinsella's head struck him in the right side and sent him hurtling over to the left, where he fell across Stapleton's prone form. A stream of blood from a severed artery in his throat flowed down over the back of Stapleton's neck.

"He's dead," said Madden, as he stooped over Murphy's body.

Kinsella crawled over and looked at the corpse.

"Take him out onto the landing," he said to Madden. "Then go downstairs and fetch Colgan to take Lynch's place."

As he crawled back to the center window, he looked over his shoulder at Lynch, who was lying on his belly beyond the doorway.

"Come and take Murphy's place," he said. "Keep well down."

Machine-gun bullets were sweeping through the room in an almost constant stream and at a low level. Yet the little newsboy was so eager to get into action that he ignored Kinsella's words of caution. He ran headlong towards the window without stooping.

"Keep down," shouted Kinsella at him.

The lad was then halfway across the floor. He was struck in the head and in the chest just as Kinsella shouted. He lurched forward and fell with his arms outstretched, like a baseball player sliding on his belly into base.

Madden dropped the corpse that he was dragging from the room. Then he reached forward and turned Lynch over on his back.

"Blood'n'ounds!" he cried, as he raised the lad's head. "This fellow is done for as well."

132

One of Lynch's eyes had been pierced. The other eye was already fixed and sightless. The heels of his boots tapped the floor a few times. Then he stiffened.

"Skinny?" Holden cried in horror. "Is Skinny dead?"

"Stone dead," Madden said. "He hardly knew what hit him."

"All right," said Kinsella. "Take him away, Madden. Look to your front, the rest of you. Move over to this window, Holden. Get back as quickly as you can, Madden."

Holden crossed himself as he crawled over to Kinsella's window.

"Lord have mercy on the poor little fellow," he said. "I'll have it on my conscience to the hour of my death that I gave him a clout, all over losing a few lousy shillings."

Madden dropped the corpses against the wall on the landing and then ran downstairs to the kitchen, where he found Tommy Colgan sitting on a chair by the back door.

"Come on upstairs," he said to the lad. "You're to take Lynch's place on the landing. He got killed."

Tommy stared fixedly at him and did not move or speak.

"Do you want me to give you a good wallop?" Madden said.

The lad still remained motionless and silent, staring fixedly at the Connemara man in the peculiarly detached manner of a person under the influence of terror.

"Come on, you disgraceful little bastard," cried Madden, as he gripped Tommy by the scruff of the neck and shook him. "Get on your feet and come along with me."

The lad clung to the seat of the chair with both hands.

"Let me go," he whispered. "Don't touch me."

Madden raised him with one hand and removed the chair with the other. Then he pushed him towards the stairs.

133

"A fine specimen you turned out to be," he growled. "I told your mother that I'd keep an eye on you, though, so I'll do it; even if I have to beat you to within an inch of your life in order to make you fight like a man. Blood'n-'ounds! If there's any drop of spunk at all left in you, I'll make you spill it. I'll see that you stand your ground and not disgrace the decent woman that bore you."

With the rage of battle in his blood, the "miraculous protector" had a very false notion of what the little woman expected from him.

"You bloody little waster!" he cried, as he thumped the lad vigorously in the back on the way upstairs. "You'll have to deal with me if you don't start fighting."

On reaching the landing, Tommy stared at the corpses fixedly, in the same peculiarly detached manner. Still looking at them, he sat down on the floor with his back to the wall.

"Stay there now," Madden said, "and do what you're bid."

Then he crouched and returned to his position, muttering to himself:

"A fellow like that would be better off dead."

He found Stapleton staring in disgust at his left palm, which was stained with blood.

"Did you get hit?" he said.

"No," said Stapleton in a matter-of-fact tone that was strangely unlike the expression of disgust on his face. "It's that other fellow's blood. My neck is covered with it. How horrible! I loathe the sight of blood. It has always made me feel ill."

The imperial troops now brought more machine guns into action and began to fan out along their right flank as well as their left, in order to reach the bank of the canal to east and west of the outpost. At the same time they crept slowly forward along the avenue, one by one, using the walls in the gardens and the trees on the pavements for cover.

"Fire only at good targets," Kinsella cautioned his men. "We haven't got much ammunition left."

Madden saw a soldier take cover behind a tree. As he took careful aim and waited for the man to move forward again, a new and ugly passion took possession of him. It came from the depths of his soul, which were now being scoured for reserves of strength to sustain the terrible strain of battle. It was a brute hatred of the man that lay hidden behind the tree; no longer his partner in a dance of death, but another animal for whose blood he lusted. The skin of his cheeks gathered, like rough stitches, about the corners of his eyes.

He fired as the man reappeared and then grunted with intense pleasure as he saw the rifle drop from the stricken soldier's hands.

"Ha!" he growled. "There's a cock that will never crow again!"

The soldier stood erect in a leisurely manner and then walked slowly across the pavement to the railing of a garden, with one hand against the breast of his tunic and the other stretched out in front of him. He doubled over as he struck the railing and lay suspended that way, with his toes touching the pavement and his hands almost within reach of the newly turned earth in a flower bed. His taut buttocks jerked spasmodically as if prodded by a needle.

"Ha!" Madden gloated, as he watched the convulsive

135

movements of his dying enemy. "That cock will never again be heard screeching at dawn of day."

His barbaric joy did not last long. It gave place to impotent rage, as the soldiers continued to advance steadily yard by yard, in spite of an occasional loss inflicted on them by the sparse fire from the insurgent rifles. Then even rage deserted him and the awareness of defeat brought querulous doubts into his mind. He had to glance over his shoulder now and again at Kinsella in order to banish them. Each time that he saw the calm detached face of his captain, his faith was renewed. The light of worship shone in his eyes and he felt a warmth in his throat. Yet the bitterness of frustration remained in his mind and his faith no longer caused him joy. It had become pregnant with tragedy. The orchestra of battle had begun to play a lament for his dance.

Daylight was now fading. The machine-gun bullets had littered the floor with plaster, torn the woodwork to shreds and pierced the rear wall with a network of large holes. The lower part of the banisters leading to the top floor had fallen on the carpet that draped the center of the stairway. Then the carpet caught fire and the flames spread to the fallen pieces of wood.

Stapleton's sensitive nostrils were the first to smell the burning. He turned his head and saw the flames.

"The stairs are on fire," he shouted.

"Colgan," Kinsella shouted, "put out that fire."

The lad did not answer.

"I'll go," said Stapleton.

"See what happened to Colgan," Kinsella called after him as he crawled to the door, "and fetch the remainder of the ammunition."

Stapleton called out from the landing that there was no sign of Colgan. Then he put out the fire and crawled back into the room with the box of ammunition. He halted and stared at Furlong when he was close to Kinsella's window.

"There's something the matter with that man," he said.

Holden crawled over to Furlong, who was lying flat on his face with his arms extended.

"God rest his soul," he cried out, after he had looked at the old soldier's face. "He got hit right in the middle of the forehead."

"Stay there, Holden," said Kinsella.

Then he looked into the box of ammunition.

"Is that the lot?" he said.

"That's all there is," said Stapleton.

"Good Lord!" said Kinsella.

They continued to fire sparingly until their rifle ammunition was exhausted. By then, night was falling fast and the imperial troops had reached the houses along the south bank of the canal, to the east of the bridge. They had also crept very close to the bridge along the avenue. Others had advanced from the west along the south bank of the canal, under cover of a low cement wall.

Kinsella distributed the remaining eighty rounds of revolver ammunition and said:

"We'll keep this until he charges the bridge. Pack up now. We must be ready to retreat in a hurry when he crosses."

Then he smiled and added in a gentle tone:

"Well done, lads."

Madden got a lump in his throat on hearing Kinsella's words of praise. The feeling of bitterness vanished from

137

his mind as he realized that the battle had really ended in victory for his "crowd," instead of defeat. He realized too, for the first time, that the fight in which he had taken part had a far more noble purpose than the lustful pleasure it had inspired in him. The beauty of the Idea that possessed him became partially unveiled. He wanted to kneel down and kiss his captain's feet, in order to express his tender joy.

It was quite dark when he hurried downstairs with Stapleton's big sack, in which they had stowed the remainder of their supplies. He had put down the sack by the back door, in readiness for their retreat, when he noticed that Tommy Colgan was again seated there.

Now he did not thump or berate the lad for having deserted his post. Instead, he touched him gently on the shoulder.

"Take it easy, now, Tommy," he said. "We'll soon be leaving here."

He had been made gentle by becoming aware of the stark beauty that makes men fight and die: in pursuit of a love they cannot possess or comprehend.

14

⊓⊔⊓⊔⊓⊔⊓⊔⊓⊔⊓⊔⊓⊔⊓⊔⊓⊔⊓⊔⊓⊔⊓⊔⊓

A FEW MINUTES after Madden's return to the drawing room, the soldiers on the avenue raised a shout and charged, under cover of intense machine-gun and rifle fire. Some of them carried buckets laden with hand grenades.

Standing behind the brickwork piers, with the empty rifles slung across their backs, the four insurgents kept firing the Mauser pistol and the three revolvers in a vain attempt to halt the mass of dim figures that ran headlong to the bridge. Again men fell as they mounted the slope, but others passed over the fallen in an ever-rolling wave, until the hump was crossed. Shouting in triumph, they fanned out on the northern side of the bridge. Some ran along the street that flanked the outpost on the west. Others took cover under the front wall and got ready to throw their hand grenades.

"Come on, lads," Kinsella shouted. "Retire."

They were crawling to the door when two grenades came through the right-hand windows. One of them burst beside Holden, killing him instantly. The other rolled through the doorway onto the landing before it exploded, shattering part of the drawing-room wall and the stairway leading to the top floor. As the three survivors groped their way along the landing, through a thick cloud of dust and smoke, several other grenades exploded in their rear. The drawing room burst into flames as they began to run downstairs.

"Open that door, Tommy," Madden shouted as they reached the kitchen, which was now in total darkness. "Hurry up."

The lad was still fumbling with the bolt when they reached him. Shouting soldiers were already forcing their way into the hall, before they managed to open the door and escape into the back yard. Madden carried the sack. Kinsella reloaded his pistol as they ran to a high wall at the far end of the garden. Then he knelt on one knee by the foot of the wall and aimed his pistol at the back door.

"Get over," he said to the others, "and wait at the far side."

Madden crouched and let Stapleton and Tommy Colgan use his back as a footstool to cross the wall. A soldier came out of the kitchen as he was throwing across the sack. The soldier fell after Kinsella had fired twice. Then Madden leaped and gripped the summit of the wall. He was raising himself with his hands when another soldier issued from the back door at a run. Kinsella fired again, making the soldier duck back hurriedly into the house. Then he gripped Madden's hand and clambered up the wall. As Madden dropped into the lane beyond, several other soldiers opened fire from the back yard. Sprawled across the top of the wall, with his legs hanging down the far side, Kinsella returned their fire.

The lane curved almost at right angles, immediately to the left of the spot where Madden landed. Stapleton was standing at the corner, with his hands on the throat of a soldier, whom he held pinned against the wall. He panted loudly as he pressed the windpipe with all his force. Madden struck the soldier three times on the top of the skull with the barrel of his revolver. The man went limp and sank down onto his buttocks against the base of the wall. Still clutching his throat, Stapleton went down with him.

Madden tried to drag Stapleton away by the shoulders.

"Let go," he shouted.

Like a dog that has his fangs embedded in a fallen enemy, Stapleton maintained his grip on the soldier's throat for a few moments. Then he collapsed, just as the soldier had done, when he was forced to abandon his grip. His legs doubled under him when Madden tried to make him stand. His whole body was limp and trembled violently.

"Blood'n'ounds!" Madden said, as Kinsella dropped into the lane. "This fellow must be hit. He can't stand."

"Carry him," said Kinsella. "I'll take the sack."

Madden hoisted Stapleton onto his back and moved off to the right. Kinsella followed, with the sack on his shoulder and his pistol in his hand.

"Get a move on, Madden," Kinsella shouted. "They're coming after us through the garden. Run as fast as you can."

Tommy Colgan had waited a short distance down the lane, looking back over his shoulder at what Stapleton and Madden were doing to the soldier. He had his hands on the ground and his right leg thrust back, like a man set for the start of a race. He took off at full speed when Madden and Kinsella approached. He was now bareheaded, having thrown away his Boer hat while crossing the garden. The rest of his uniform was partly hidden by a raincoat that he had found hanging from a peg in the kitchen. It belonged to a short fat woman servant. It hung loose about his slender body, but the sleeves and skirt were ludicrously short, reaching only to his elbows and the upper part of his thighs.

The lane ran due east for forty yards. They had almost reached the far end when they were fired upon by a soldier from the top of the garden wall. Three other soldiers came round the angle of the lane and opened fire. Tommy Colgan and Madden turned into a wide street and ran towards the north. Kinsella waited at the corner for a few moments to fire back at the soldiers, who were now coming along the lane in pursuit of the fugitives. The soldiers dropped to the ground. Then Kinsella ran after his comrades.

They went north for two hundred yards and then turned to the west. Kinsella looked back as he turned. The soldiers had abandoned the pursuit. They turned north again into a long lane and slackened their pace. There was heavy firing in the distance, to east and west and north, but the neighborhood was quiet. The lane was deserted, except for a solitary drunken man who lay asleep in a doorway.

Kinsella called on them to halt on reaching a hole in a blank wall, near the far end of the lane. He looked through the hole and saw a waste plot that was littered with rubbish.

"We'll go in here and take a look at Stapleton," he said to Madden.

Madden followed Kinsella through the hole and laid Stapleton down carefully against the foot of the wall.

142

"Blood'n'ounds!" he said. "It's true for the old proverb. Even a hen feels heavy at the end of a long journey."

Three goats were tethered to a rusty boiler in the center of the plot. They began to bleat on seeing the intruders. Then they pressed forward to the end of their ropes, snorting and with their tails laid flat along their backs.

Kinsella examined Stapleton and said:

"He's not wounded."

"He's not?" said Madden. "Then what ails him?"

He tried to prop Stapleton against the wall in a sitting position. Stapleton fell over to the right, with his head lolling lifelessly and his mouth open in a grotesque leer.

"See that?" Madden said. "He has no life in him at all. You could tie knots with his arms and legs. He's shaking like a leaf."

He tried again to make Stapleton sit erect, but without success.

"He keeps slipping like a corpse," he said.

"Did we take the bottle of brandy with us?" said Kinsella.

"It's in the bag," said Madden.

"Get it," said Kinsella.

Madden took the bottle from the sack and opened it with Kinsella's penknife. Then they raised Stapleton's head and poured a little of the brandy into his mouth. He began to splutter as soon as the fiery liquor touched his palate. He pawed the air blindly for a few moments. Then he swallowed what he had in his mouth, shook himself, grasped the bottle with both hands and began to drink in great long gulps.

"Take it easy," Madden said.

He snatched the bottle and gave it to Kinsella.

143

"Have a drop, sir," he said. "It must be a powerful creature, sure enough. That lad was earning his death and one good jorum of it cured him."

Stapleton had, indeed, recovered with amazing speed. He now rubbed his eyes, looked about wildly and tried to rise.

"Sit still, man," said Madden, pushing him down again.

"My God!" said Stapleton. "What happened? Where am I?"

"You're all right now," said Madden. "You were nearly in the other world but you came back. Take it easy."

"By Jove!" said Kinsella, as he handed back the bottle to Madden. "I had no idea that I was so tired."

He threw himself down against the wall, let his arms hang down between his thighs, closed his eyes and dropped his chin onto his chest.

"How horrible!" said Stapleton, as he looked into the distance. "I now remember it all."

Madden took a long pull at the bottle and then offered it to Tommy, who was sitting apart.

"Come and have a sup of this," he said in a drowsy tone.

The brandy had intoxicated his exhausted body almost at once. His haggard face glowed and he was grinning.

"Come on," he continued, as the lad did not move. "This powerful creature will warm the cockles of your little heart."

Tommy stared at Madden in a hostile fashion and then shook his head, like a stray dog that has attached itself to some people for protection and yet holds aloof from them, suspicious of their attempts to make friends with it.

"I choked him," Stapleton cried out in a loud voice.

Kinsella raised his head, looked at Stapleton and said in a tired voice:

"Do keep quiet, George."

"I must tell you what happened," Stapleton said.

"Not now, George," said Kinsella.

"I must speak," said Stapleton. "I really was not responsible for what I did."

"Be quiet," said Kinsella. "We must go on again in a few minutes. Be silent and let us rest."

"I simply must speak, Michael," said Stapleton.

Kinsella again closed his eyes, dropped his head and whispered:

"All right, then. Go ahead but don't shout."

Stapleton asked Madden for the bottle.

"Arrah! You've had enough already, man," Madden said, grinning from ear to ear. "It's gone to your head."

"Just a little, please," said Stapleton. "My mouth is very dry."

"Not more than a single little slug," said Madden, as he passed the bottle. "Just enough to wet the tip of your tongue."

Stapleton shuddered after he had drunk. Then he returned the bottle to Madden and looked into the distance.

"You've no head for drink," Madden said jovially, as he gave Stapleton a friendly thump in the side. "A man like you, that talks such a lot, ought never touch a drop."

"It was very odd," said Stapleton in a low detached voice. "When I dropped into the lane, we bumped into each other. He had just come around the corner, holding his rifle and bayonet across his chest. He could easily have stabbed me, after he had staggered back a little. I was

145

unarmed. You see, I had lost my revolver leaving the room. I dropped it when I was thrown to the floor by the explosions. In any case, even if I were armed, I was too surprised to defend myself, had he cared to kill me at that first moment of our meeting. However, he felt just as embarrassed as I was myself. We were like two strangers that collide on a street. They stare at one another and then apologize, both together. I'm positive that I intended to apologize when I raised my hands. You know the sort of awkward gesture one makes, when one stumbles into someone. One touches an arm, or a shoulder, as one raises one's hat and says: 'So sorry.' Yet I took him by the throat instead of offering an apology. That is what I cannot understand or forgive. Then I pushed him against the wall, kicked him in the stomach with my knee and strangled him. I swear to you that I was not in the least conscious of what I was doing. Far from it. To choke a fellow creature with one's hands, especially a man like myself who loves to play the piano . . . "

"Arrah! What's all that talk about choking?" Madden interrupted in a jovial tone. "Sure, you couldn't choke a flea, man alive."

"Have you got any ammunition left, Madden?" Kinsella asked, with his eyes closed.

Madden searched his pockets and said:

"I have eight rounds."

"Load your revolver," said Kinsella. "We must be going now."

"We kept looking at one another in horror while it was happening," said Stapleton, "as if it were a third person that was doing it to us both. We both shared the agony. I feel sure of that."

146

"Oh, stop talking about something you never did," said Madden, as he loaded his revolver. "You didn't choke that man at all."

"What do you mean?" said Stapleton in an arrogant tone, as he looked at Madden. "I know I choked him."

"If you had choked him," Madden said, "he'd be dead."

"He was dead," said Stapleton. "I saw his dead eyes when I fell on top of him."

"Sure, he was dead when you fell on him," Madden said, "but it was I killed him."

"You?" said Stapleton.

"I killed him, all right," Madden said. "I cracked his skull with this revolver and down he went."

"Was it really you?" said Stapleton.

"Arrah!" said Madden. "Have sense, little man. It would take stronger hands than yours to choke a big strong soldier."

Then he looked at Kinsella and said respectfully:

"It's loaded now, sir."

Kinsella staggered to his feet and said:

"Come on, lads."

"You have lovely little hands like a lady," Madden said to Stapleton, as he jumped to his feet. "They couldn't choke a rabbit. It takes powerful hands to knock the breath out of a man's throat."

He took another good pull at the bottle before putting it into his pocket.

"Blood'n'ounds!" he cried with enthusiasm, as he swung the big sack onto his shoulder. "That parliament is worth every penny of the money it costs."

Then he set his cap at a rakish angle and strode out into the lane, swaying at the hips and swinging his free arm,

147

like a tipsy fellow strutting boastfully from a tavern to challenge anyone that cared to fight him.

Stapleton caught him by the arm after they had gone a short way along the lane to the right.

"It doesn't help me in the least," he whispered tensely, "to know that you killed him. It makes no difference who was ultimately responsible for his death."

"What's that?" Madden said drowsily.

He was beginning to feel terribly sleepy. The brandy he had drunk was no longer able to hold back the lassitude that follows battle.

"The important thing," said Stapleton, "is that I tried to strangle him. It makes no difference that it was you . . ."

"Arrah! Stop boasting about something you didn't do," Madden interrupted. "Blood'n'ounds! Little fellows like yourself are all the same. They are always trying to draw attention to themselves and laying claim to the work of better men."

He staggered to the right and almost fell as he stepped from the pavement into the roadway. When he righted himself, he had to clutch the sack with both hands, in order to keep it from slipping down his back. The muscles of his arms were reluctant to exercise their power.

"I'm not boasting," said Stapleton indignantly. "Good Lord! I'm horrified by what I did."

With a great effort, Madden hoisted the sack higher up on his shoulder. Then he stooped low, in order to let his back carry the weight independently of his sleepy arms.

"Of course you're boasting," he said, as he staggered forward with his eyes half-closed. "You might as well try to knock out Jack Johnson with one blow of your little fist.

148

You couldn't choke a man with those hands of yours, even if you kept trying for a whole year."

"Silence," Kinsella called back over his shoulder.

Madden shuddered with pleasure as he heard his captain's voice.

"Ah! Lord God!" he said to himself with enthusiasm. "There's a man for you. He has no equal on God's earth."

Hunger and thirst now began to plague him, in addition to his weariness. Yet these torments were unable to dull the intense satisfaction that he felt as he stumbled forward slowly towards the same bridge that he had crossed on the way south, fresh and eager like a hound that strains at its leash after a coursing hare.

Weariness, hunger and thirst were merely superficial cravings, which could easily be cured. The satisfaction lay deep down in his soul, which had been purged by the medicine of battle. All the unavenged insults that rankled there had been swept away.

Henceforth that satisfaction would always be there, deep down in his soul; the exultant satisfaction of the slave that has freed himself from resentment by taking up arms and going forth to do battle for the Idea of freedom.

15

`⊓⊔⊓⊔⊓⊔⊓⊔⊓⊔⊓⊔⊓⊔⊓⊔⊓⊔⊓⊔⊓⊔⊓⊔⊓⊔`

Having crossed the bridge safely, in spite of continuous heavy fire from the south side of the river, they crawled westwards towards O'Connell Street under cover of the quay wall. Then they ran across the roadway into a street that led due north. After going about ten yards through this street, they turned west into a lane that ran parallel with the quays. The door of a house on the northern side of the lane was open. In order to take shelter from heavy fire that raked the lane from the east, they dashed through the doorway. Then they followed Kinsella down the dark hallway to a faint glimmer of light that came from the bottom of a door at the far end. Pistol in hand, he threw open the door and entered a shabby kitchen. The others staggered after him.

A man in Volunteer uniform was crouching over a bare deal table that stood in the center of the room. His right cheek was resting on his crossed arms when the fugitives entered. He raised his head slowly and looked at them. There was a crazed expression in his bloodshot blue eyes. His sallow face looked ghastly in the light of a shaded paraffin lamp that hung low over the table from a chain attached to the ceiling. His right hand was covered with bloodstained bandages.

150

"Ye are too late now," he cried angrily. "He's dead."

Kinsella came over to the table and picked up a jug that stood there. He looked into it eagerly. It was empty.

"Any water here?" he said to the sallow-faced man.

"I brought him in here an hour ago," said the sallow-faced man, "looking for someone to stop the bleeding."

Kinsella threw himself down on a chair and laid his forehead against the table.

"See can you find some water, Madden," he muttered.

"Yes, sir," said Madden.

He threw his sack on the floor and went round the table towards the sink, taking the jug with him.

"I couldn't do anything for him myself," shouted the sallow-faced man, as he thrust out his wounded hand. "Not a bloody thing could I do, with all the fingers of my right hand smashed on me."

Stapleton sat down beside Kinsella and looked at the sallow-faced man intently. Tommy Colgan walked stealthily to the fireplace and sat down on a three-legged stool before the grate, in which the remains of a fire were still glowing. He crossed his arms on his chest and rocked himself. His teeth chattered.

"There was a woman here when we came," cried the sallow-faced man, now addressing his remarks to Stapleton. "She got frightened when she saw us and ran out screeching, with a child in her shawl. I could do nothing for Frank, I tell you. Not a cursed thing could I do. The blood kept pouring out of him until he died."

Having slaked his thirst at the tap, Madden filled the jug and brought it to Kinsella, together with a cup that he took from the dresser.

151

"Blood'n'ounds!" he said. "I never before had such a thirst."

"Don't swear in a house of the dead," the sallow-faced man shouted angrily. "Have you no shame in you?"

"I see no dead man here," Madden said.

The sallow-faced man pointed to a corpse that lay stretched on a ragged black sofa against the far wall, to the left of the dresser.

"Huh?" Madden said. "Is that man dead? I thought he was asleep."

"It's all that's now left of Frank Lamont," said the sallow-faced man, "one of the greatest hurlers that ever drew on a ball in mid-field."

Madden took the bottle of brandy from his pocket as he walked over to the corpse.

"He played four years for his county," said the sallow-faced man, who had now begun to sob freely. "Then he went over to Liverpool, to work as a clerk for the shipping firm that employed me as a messenger. Him and me became pals in the Volunteers. He was my company captain. As fine a man as ever walked God's earth."

Madden opened the bottle and took a long pull. Then he stooped and examined an automatic pistol that lay in a holster attached to the dead man's belt. It was a beautiful new weapon of American make.

"That's a fine gun he had, 'faith," he said in a voice that was hoarse with greed. "By Ganeys! That looks like the king of all guns."

"What are you doing with it?" shouted the sallow-faced man.

"I'm just looking at it," Madden said.

152

"Leave it alone," shouted the sallow-faced man. "It belongs to Frank."

"How could it belong to him and he dead?" said Madden.

"Never mind," cried the sallow-faced man. "He was a soldier and a dead soldier has a right to his gun. Don't you touch it."

Madden drew in a deep breath through his nostrils as he put the pistol back into its holster. Then he came back to the table and handed the bottle to Kinsella. Excited by the possibility of possessing the beautiful new American pistol and by the fresh draught of brandy he had drunk, he no longer felt weary. There was a broad grin on his face.

"Now that your throat is wet, sir," he said to Kinsella, "you might be able to swallow another little sup of this creature."

Stapleton thrust the drinking cup towards Kinsella.

"Let me have some, too," he said.

Madden picked up the sack, put it on the table and began to open it.

"Frank left a wife and three children behind him in Liverpool," said the sallow-faced man, "and he could hardly sleep a wink from worrying about them, while we were hiding out at Kimmage, with the crowd that came over from England for the rising. Ah! The poor creatures will never see him again now. God rest his soul! Me and him were fighting since Monday in a house on the quays. Little I thought, when he put that bandage on my hand this morning, that I wouldn't be able to . . ."

He stopped speaking suddenly and gaped at the food that

Madden was taking from the sack. His lunatic face no longer showed any sign of regret for his dead comrade. Indeed, he had completely forgotten the silent man that lay stretched out stiff on the ragged black sofa, with his toes bolt upright and his hands crossed on his chest.

"Meat!" he cried, slavering at the mouth like a famished animal. "Oh! Lord God! Look at all the meat."

"Come on, lads," Madden shouted exultantly. "Have at it. Blood'n'ounds! We have earned it."

He and the sallow-faced man began to eat in feverish haste, stuffing ham and cheese and butter and eggs and biscuits into their mouths promiscuously. They swallowed large morsels of these diverse stuffs pell-mell, almost without putting a tooth to them. Kinsella and Stapleton used more restraint. Indeed, Kinsella appeared to be in the last stages of exhaustion and ate very little. Stapleton was much more alert. There was a wolfish look in his brilliant blue eyes, even though he nibbled daintily at each morsel. All four of them ate in silence for several minutes.

Then Kinsella turned to Tommy Colgan and said:

"Come and have something to eat, Colgan."

The lad had been watching the table furtively over his shoulder ever since the food appeared. Yet he had not approached. Although tormented by hunger, he was unable to conquer the fear that kept him aloof from his comrades. He turned away hurriedly on being addressed and drew his stool closer to the fire. Then he raised the collar of his skimpy raincoat, like a woman trying to conceal the beauty of her face from the eyes of a lecherous stranger.

Kinsella rose from the table and walked slowly over to the fireplace. A reddish stubble now covered his jaws and his somber eyes had become soft with compassion, giving

154

his haggard face a stark beauty, like that of a hermit monk contemplating a vision.

He went on one knee beside the lad and touched him gently on the arm.

"Listen, Colgan," he whispered softly. "You mustn't feel ashamed of yourself, or think that I'm angry with you for the way you behaved today. I couldn't possibly be angry with you for being afraid, because I behaved in the same way myself, more or less, after I heard last Sunday that the rising had been postponed. I went back to my lodgings, took off my uniform and hid it in a cupboard, together with everything else that had any connection with the Volunteer movement. Then I got into bed and covered my head. I was terribly afraid for a long time, as I lay thinking of what might have happened had the rising taken place that evening. Yet I didn't feel in the least afraid next morning when a man came for me. By that time, you see, I had conquered my fear by an effort of will. I put on my uniform again and went out to fight. I've not been in the least afraid since then. When you told me that you were ill, I knew at once that you felt exactly the same way that I had felt last Sunday. Yet I had to be severe with you under the circumstances. Later, when I saw you throw away your hat in the garden and noticed that you had taken that raincoat, I wanted to talk to you; but again I didn't have an opportunity of doing so. You see, I understood that you were trying to hide your uniform, just as I had done myself, and that you could overcome your fear by making the same effort of will that I made. I feel certain that you have courage. Otherwise, you would not have taken up arms, when much stronger men than you stayed at home dishonorably. Neither did you run away since then, even though you could easily have done so."

He paused, tightened his grip on the lad's arm and added with great emphasis:

"This I know for certain and you must believe me. There is no fear that a courageous man cannot master by an effort of will. Come now, lad. Make the effort. Face your fear boldly and then you won't have to feel ashamed any more."

Tommy had begun to tremble slightly after listening to the first few words. Now he turned suddenly, grasped Kinsella's hand and pressed it against his forehead.

"All right, lad," Kinsella whispered. "Come to the table. Sit down with the others and have some food."

Tommy rose and approached the table slowly, walking almost on tiptoe and glancing furtively at the three men who were sitting there, as if he were afraid they might attack him. Then he suddenly dropped into the chair that Kinsella had occupied and began to eat ravenously. As soon as the first morsel touched his palate, he forgot his fear as completely as the sallow-faced man had forgotten his dead comrade. His eyes became fierce. He gulped the food wholesale, crouched low over the board and breathing heavily through his nostrils.

Kinsella stood watching the lad for a little while. Then he walked slowly over to the black sofa on which the corpse lay stretched. With his arms folded on his chest he looked down at the dead man's face.

His own face had again become somber. The vision had given place to the loneliness of incomprehension.

16

‌⊓⊔⊓⊔⊓⊔⊓⊔⊓⊔⊓⊔⊓⊔⊓⊔⊓⊔⊓⊔⊓⊔⊓⊔⊓

S‌UDDENLY there was a booming sound that was followed almost at once by a resounding crash.

"Blood'n'ounds!" Madden said, as he looked towards the door. "What was that? It didn't sound like thunder."

"Artillery," said Stapleton. "Quite close range, too. We heard the explosion almost at the same time as the discharge."

"Jesus, Mary and Joseph!" said the sallow-faced man, crossing himself hurriedly. "If he's brought out his big guns, then our goose is cooked and make no mistake about it. It's Lord have mercy on us now and we faced with a who-dare-spoil like that."

Tommy Colgan had half risen to his feet on hearing the sound of the explosion, obeying an instinctive impulse to seek refuge in flight. Then he looked at Kinsella and cut the impulse short. Remembering what his commander had just urged him to do, he forced himself back onto his chair and tried to continue his meal. Three more shells burst, almost instantaneously, as he was putting another morsel of food to his lips. In spite of all his efforts, he dropped the morsel to the board and began to tremble violently. It seemed to him that a great weight was pressing against the pit of his stomach. He wanted terribly to cry out for

157

help to Kinsella, who was then walking across the floor from the sofa to the door. He had to grip his lower lip fiercely with his teeth to prevent himself from shouting.

"I'll go and have a look," said Kinsella as he went out into the hall.

"I knew he would use artillery," said Stapleton, in the tone of a man that is very pleased with himself. "Can you imagine? Both Connolly and Pearse were fully persuaded that he wouldn't. I heard them both maintain, at my aunt's house one evening, that the government would not want to injure the property of rich loyalist citizens and would refrain on that account from resorting to artillery bombardment. That, of course, was a most childish idea. Literary people, no matter how brilliant, are always childish . . ."

His words were drowned by a crash that was infinitely louder than the previous ones. A shell had burst in the immediate neighborhood of the room, whose flimsy walls shook violently. A wide crack appeared at a corner of the ceiling and began to advance towards the iron hook to which the lamp chain was attached.

"All government is based on violence," Stapleton was saying imperturbably, when his voice again became audible. "It will use violence, to the fullest extent of which it is capable, in order to maintain itself in power, irrespective of . . ."

"Shut your mouth," Madden cried as he jumped to his feet. "The captain must have been near where that . . ."

"Look out for the lamp," shouted the sallow-faced man, as he also rose. "It's going to fall down."

The crack had reached the hook, which broke away from the ceiling and let the lamp fall. Madden caught it deftly before it touched the board. He put it down carefully and then made for the door at a run.

"Jesus, Mary and Joseph!" said the sallow-faced man, as he again crossed himself. "There's no hope for us now."

Dragging his legs like a paralyzed person, Tommy Colgan moved away to the far end of the table, clutching the edge of the board with his widespread hands.

"A government is really a complex kind of animal," said Stapleton, as he stared into the distance with a vague smile on his face. "The various groups of citizens are its limbs and organs. Just as a wounded animal will bite off its foot . . ."

"Are you badly hurt, sir?" Madden cried out in the doorway.

Kinsella staggered into the room, as several more shells burst in rapid succession to the south along the quays. His face was deadly pale. His uniform was covered with dust. The right sleeve of his tunic was torn. He thrust aside the hand that Madden put on his shoulder.

"Come on, lads," he muttered in an exhausted tone. "Get out of here. He has reached the south bank of the river and brought his artillery into action. He may be going to attack headquarters at once."

The sallow-faced man had rushed from the table before Kinsella finished speaking.

"Jesus, Mary and Joseph!" he yelled as he bolted through the door.

Kinsella refused to drink from the brandy bottle that Madden fetched from the table.

"Pack up that food," he said. "Be quick."

"What happened, Michael?" said Stapleton, as he and Kinsella followed Colgan into the hallway. "You look ill."

"A shell burst beside me," said Kinsella, "when I was running back into the house. Then the wall fell on top of me."

Madden was scooping the remains of the food from the table into the mouth of his sack when the sallow-faced man shouted from the hallway:

"The hall door is blocked and there is no back way. We're trapped in this bloody place."

Madden thrust the brandy bottle into his jacket pocket, hoisted the sack onto his shoulder and ran to the door.

"Blood'n'ounds!" he muttered as he reached it. "I almost forgot that dead man's gun."

He turned about, ran to the couch and stripped the corpse of its fine officer's belt, to which the holstered pistol and a haversack stuffed with ammunition were attached. He put the loot into his sack and again ran across the floor. As he passed the table, a shell burst directly overhead. The cracked ceiling fell. A large piece of mortar struck the sack and sent him sprawling out into the hallway on his face. He was almost stunned by the blow and the fall. As he lay motionless for a few moments to regain his breath, he felt awed by the power of the colossus that was now hurling thunderbolts at him from beyond the river, like the giants in the fairy tales he had heard about the hearth fires of his native village on winter nights. As he moved in order to rise, however, his limbs smarted and his awe of the colossus changed to furious anger. He leaped to his feet shouting curses and eager to do battle with his monstrous enemy.

At that moment the hallway was in pitch darkness. The air was full of acrid smoke and dust, which made the other four men cough as they struggled to make an exit.

160

"We're trapped," the sallow-faced man kept shouting. "We'll die in here as sure as God."

As Madden put aside his sack, however, the darkness was suddenly dispelled. The lamp had been upset when the ceiling fell. The oil had poured out onto the table and caught fire. Then the table burst into flames, which were now darting up and out in all directions, making the myriad particles of dust that floated on the air shimmering like jewels. Their radiance flowed into the hallway.

"Fire! Fire!" screamed the sallow-faced man. "Oh! Mother of God! We'll be burned alive in here."

As soon as there was light, Madden spat on his hands and plunged forward to the mound of rubble, at which the others had been clawing impotently until then.

"Get out of my way," he shouted. "I'll soon make a hole."

He hurled himself at the rubble, after the manner of a terrier digging out a grounded rat. In a few minutes, he had made a hole through which a man could crawl. By then the flames had enveloped the whole kitchen and their roar vied with the sound of the shells that continued to explode in the neighborhood at frequent intervals.

"Out ye go now," Madden shouted, as he returned to his sack.

The sallow-faced man was the first to crawl through the hole. Tommy Colgan went next. Kinsella was almost powerless and had to be dragged on his belly by Stapleton. By the time they had gone through, the flames had begun to thrust their stabbing tongues into the hallway and to curl about the doorjambs.

As Madden was about to stoop, in order to go through the hole, he remembered the brandy bottle. He put his

161

hand on the jacket pocket in which he had stowed it. Then he grinned with pleasure on finding that it had not been broken by the fall. He was again going to stoop when it occurred to him that it would be better to drink what was left of the liquor, then and there, rather than run the risk of losing it through some other misadventure of the same sort. Thereupon he took out the bottle, pulled the cork with his teeth, wiped his lips with the back of his hand, spread his legs, leaned back and began to drink.

"Come on, Madden," Kinsella called to him from the lane.

Madden took the bottle from his lips and shouted:

"Coming, sir. Be right with you."

Then he cleared his throat, put the bottle to his lips once more and continued to drink with full-bellied satisfaction. The flames had now enveloped the rear end of the hallway and were advancing with a mighty roar, as if consciously seeking to devour him. Yet he went on drinking at leisure, savoring every drop of the intoxicating nectar that passed down his wide-open gullet, until no more was left. Then he sighed, smacked his lips, shook his head, threw aside the empty bottle, set his cap at a rakish angle, uttered a wild yell of defiance at the colossus and crawled through the hole.

"Here I am, sir," he said on reaching the pavement.

The sallow-faced man had disappeared, having taken to headlong flight on reaching the pavement.

"Come on, lads," said Kinsella.

He led them along the lane towards the west, keeping close to the houses on the northern side for cover, since stray bullets were still coming from the east. He was barely able to walk. He held himself very erect and thrust

162

forward his legs uncertainly, at irregular intervals, like a very dignified person in a state of intoxication. Madden tried to take him by the arm and support him, but he again thrust aside the offered help. He was breathing loudly through his nostrils and his eyes had become bloodshot.

Like rabbits flushed from a warren by a ferret, people were fleeing northwards from the quays, in terror of the bursting shells. Some of them were in their night clothes. Several of the houses that faced the river were already on fire. A building at the angle of Lower O'Connell Street and the quayside was crowned by a majestic cloud of smoke, through which a great shower of bright sparks and tongues of flame kept shooting towards the sky.

After going a short distance westwards, the four insurgents reached a narrow passageway that ran northwards from the quays, breasting the rear of the houses in the southeast block of Lower O'Connell Street. There they met a party of revelers that were in flight from a quayside tavern, where they had been carousing since Monday. Four young men were hauling a cart that was laden with cases of beer and whiskey. A little old man was also in the cart, seated on some cases of liquor. The revelers had found him outside the tavern and given him a lift. Three young women brought up the rear, marching arm in arm and singing drunkenly at the top of their voices.

As the insurgents passed the cart in the passageway, the three young women waggled their hips, did a little shuffle with their feet and broke into the chorus of their song:

> *Come, come, come to me, Thora.*
> *Come back again and be . . .*

Then the little old man stood up in the cart and ad-

163

dressed the insurgents in a most vehement manner. His words were unintelligible owing to the noise. He was dressed solely in a white cotton nightshirt that reached to his naked little feet and a tasseled red nightcap. His moon-shaped face was encircled by a luxuriant white beard that left his rosy chin exposed. He carried an alarm clock in one hand and a small carpetbag in the other. He brandished the alarm clock in a hostile fashion at the insurgents while he spoke. Swaying to and fro uncertainly, he continued to shout and to brandish his cloak until the cart had passed from sight into Lower Abbey Street.

Kinsella led his men through a small door set in a large metal gate on the western side of the passageway, in the wake of two other insurgents that were in flight from a house on the quays. Then the whole party stumbled in semidarkness to the front of the building they had entered. There they climbed a broad stairway to a restaurant on the second floor.

It was then shortly after midnight.

17

THE RESTAURANT was very large, with a lofty ceiling. It covered the whole extent of the building. Its windows opened both on Lower O'Connell Street and on the passageway to the rear. The stairhead was in the center of the floor. The tables were still laid for lunch, just as they had been when the staff hurriedly evacuated the place shortly after noon on Monday. The insurgents that came there later merely barricaded the windows and bored holes through the side walls for their interior line of communication.

Shells were falling at frequent intervals in the two buildings to the south. They were both on fire. The roar of the flames sounded in the restaurant like the harsh murmur of shellfish crawling about under weed-covered rocks on a seashore at low tide. Their reflection cast a faint glow, like fading twilight, about the immediate neighborhood of the hole in the southern wall. As each shell burst this glow became a brilliant flash, which enveloped the whole center of the room for a brief moment. The white tablecloths, the cutlery, the glasses, the plates, the cruet stands and the polished brasses of the stairhead gave an illusion of peace and comfort at these moments; like the recollections of lost youth that come in melancholy beauty to torture the mind of a sick old man, as he lies awake at night in apprehension of approaching death.

As the fugitives entered, a group of about fifteen men, all of them in a state of extreme agitation, were shifting back and forth, between the stairhead and the hole in the southern wall, making violent gestures and shouting at the top of their voices.

A very short and thin man, wearing a loose brown overcoat over the uniform of a Volunteer captain, was trying to pacify them. He kept rising on his toes and holding up his arm, like a policeman on traffic duty, as he spoke. He had a face like a bird, with a short pointed nose and wide-open blue eyes, whose glance darted hither and thither restlessly. His voice, too, was like that of a scolding bird, being excited and querulous.

"Take it easy, lads," he cried. "His artillery can't do us any harm. It's all a bluff, this firing. He has only a few old field pieces planted on the other side of the river and a gunboat down in the harbor. He didn't know what else to do, after the hiding we've given him since Monday. All we have to do is to stick it until our men arrive from the country. There's a big army on its way from the south. Another one is coming from the west. They should be here any minute now."

A huge man with a bull neck and a brick-red face, wearing the uniform of the Citizen Army, stood in front of the little officer and stamped on the floor with his heavy hobnailed boots. He carried a small sledgehammer in his right hand and a grenade in his left.

"What's the sense in handing us that bloody cod?" he shouted. "We all know there's nobody coming to help us from the country. We're not afraid of his artillery. All

166

we're asking is to be led out to fight like men and not wait here to be pounded into bits, like cattle in a pen."

Several men then shouted in unison:

"We want to fight. We want to charge the guns."

"Take it easy!" cried the little officer, rising and falling on his toes and heels, like a boxer flexing his leg muscles before the opening round of a bout in the ring. "All our positions are holding out south of the river. We're winning. All we have to do is stick it a little while longer, until the country lads . . . "

His voice was drowned by that of a large man, with prominent upper teeth, who cried out in a voice that was hysterical with impotent rage:

"We of the Citizen Army were fools to join these bloody nationalists, that are only good for making speeches and crossing themselves like monks. We should have gone out on our own and raised the Red Flag and called on the toilers of all lands to revolt against war and capitalism. Then we wouldn't be here now, like rats in a trap, isolated from our class . . . "

The bull-necked man again stamped his foot and shouted:

"Come on, lads. Follow me. We'll go out and charge across the bridge and capture those big guns, or die in the attempt."

The foolhardiness of this proposal produced the silence which the officer's exhortations had not been able to achieve. They all knew that the houses along the south bank of the river were now occupied by machine gunners of the imperial army and that even a rat could not cross the bridge unscathed. Sobered by having their helplessness brought home to them, through realization of the only alternative to their oppressive inactivity, they broke up into little groups and moved away to the western side of the room, still arguing in low voices.

Kinsella told his three comrades to rest and then went with the other officer to an alcove. There they sat down at a small table, on which there was a lighted candle stuck in the neck of an empty beer bottle.

"Come on, lads," Madden said in a jovial tone to Colgan and Stapleton.

He had stood listening to the argument with a broad grin on his face without being at all interested in what he heard. In the strange world that he now inhabited with his Idea, neither hope nor fear had any place. He had been carried aloft by "the ecstasy of the warrior" into the upper firmament, where the whirring wings of the wild geese made the only sound that broke the silence of starlit empty space.

"In this historical period of the world revolution," cried a voice, as the three men crossed the floor, "the working class is too weak to bear the brunt of the struggle alone. It must unite with all who are opposed to the imperialist war and present a solid front of . . . "

Madden threw himself down on the floor by the northern wall. Tommy Colgan and Stapleton sat on either side of him.

"They don't understand," said Stapleton in a querulous tone. "It's really strange that they should fail to understand the purpose of their gesture."

Grinning broadly, Madden stretched out his legs to their full length along the floor and placed the sack between his thighs. Then he looked at Stapleton with affection.

"Shut your mouth now and rest," he said. "It's all hours

of the night. It's time for a little fellow like yourself to be quiet. Blood'n'ounds! When I saw you first, I thought you weren't worth the ten of clubs. Now, though, if I were a king, I'd give you my finest herd of horses and my queen. Cripes! That was great work you did during the fight."

Stapleton looked at him and said in a forlorn tone:

"It's so sad that their beauty should be unknown to them."

"Lord God!" Madden said. "There must be powerful marrow in your tiny bones and you daring to squeeze a big soldier's throat, trying to jerk the life out of him with your lady's hands. Blood'n'ounds! You have great spunk in you. Stretch out your legs now, comrade, and close your eyes and rest until the captain calls us."

"This is a poetic gesture," said Stapleton in an arrogant tone, as he stretched out his legs in obedience to Madden's command. "It can only end in death, like the dance of love performed by those scarlet insects that whirl in the sunlight above a shining stream, for the few hours of their existence."

As he rested his head on his curved arms and closed his eyes, three shells burst in unison immediately to the south. The combined sound of their explosion was of a monstrous force. The center of the room became suffused with a lurid glare for more than a second.

"Any other purpose would be vulgar and meaningless," Stapleton whispered, as he began to breathe heavily with advancing sleep.

"Fire, you bastard, fire," Madden yelled in ecstasy.

With his head thrown back against the wall and his mouth open, he exulted in the fury of the colossus, now

169

hurling its thunderbolts in such reckless frenzy. He recalled the roadway speckled with the yellow slain and to
him this fury of the colossus was in answer to that
slaughter. The colossus was pursuing him, Bartly Madden,
personally, in an attempt to get revenge for those hundreds
of yellow limbs that had been severed in glorious battle.
Blood'n'ounds! The dark rapture that a man felt at sea
on a hooker in a raging gale was paltry compared to this
divine ecstasy.

He reached out with his left hand, grasped Tommy Colgan's right arm, closed his eyes and broke into song:

> *Five hundred men lay drunk all together*
> *In Tom Daly's at . . .*

Tommy Colgan interrupted the song by brusquely pulling away his arm. Madden opened his eyes, leaned forward and looked at the lad. Tommy was sitting with his
back to the wall and his hands between his hunched-up
knees. His lips were shut tightly and he was breathing
heavily through his nostrils. He stared at Madden with
hatred in his intense blue eyes.

"What ails you now in God's name?" Madden said.

"Leave me alone," Tommy said between his teeth.

Then he edged away a few inches to the left along the
floor, by waggling his rump, keeping his eyes still fixed
on Madden.

"Hell to your rotten soul," Madden said.

Then he looked at the sack, grinned and licked his
lower lip, as he thought of his loot. He removed the two
rifles that were slung across his back and laid them on
the floor, between himself and Tommy Colgan.

"That's my rifle," Tommy said in a spiteful tone, as he

170

pointed to one of the weapons. "You have no right to it. Give it to me."

Madden cursed under his breath and tossed the rifle to the lad.

"Take it and be damned to you," he said, "although it's little good a coward like yourself will get out of it."

Then he plunged his hand into the sack and took out the dead man's belt, to which the holstered pistol and the haversack were attached. He fondled the smoothly polished leather of the belt and of the holster; just as he had fondled the Lancer's rifle in the doorway of the bank. His eyes grew soft with tenderness.

"Yerrah! Lord God!" he muttered hoarsely. "There's leather for you."

Tommy took his recovered rifle in his arms and then continued to edge away on his rump along the floor, towards the hole in the northern wall. He kept his eyes fixed warily on Madden, until the bursting of another shell to the south. Then he stiffened and looked to his front. The glare made him wince and it seemed for a moment, by the dropping of his lower lip and the quivering of his nostrils, that he was going into a panic. Yet he did not do so. On the contrary, he threw his rifle across his body in a position of combat, with his left hand forward on the barrel and his right hand clutching the small of the stock behind the trigger guard. Then he continued his terribly slow journey along the floor to the left, moving jerkily like a worm and pausing after each movement. He kept his eyes now fixed on the hole in the southern wall and his features bore an expression of spiteful defiance; he was like a boy that is vowing vengeance in his soul for unjust punishment he is receiving from an elder.

171

On reaching the edge of the northern hole, he glanced back at Madden. The Connemara man had now donned the fine officer's belt and he was sitting bolt upright against the wall, arranging the shoulder strap. His bronzed face bore an expression of childish delight and abstraction. Certain that there was no danger of interference from that quarter, the lad put his right hand on the floor behind his hip, intending to rise and flee through the hole, away from the thunder of the explosions and the recurring glare of the flames. Above all, he wanted to get away from his comrades who had been witness to his shame during the battle. As his hand touched the floor, however, an impulse that he could not resist made him pause and look towards the alcove, where Kinsella was sitting at a table, listening to the excited remarks of the officer with the birdlike face. Then he trembled from head to foot and a lump came into his throat, as he caught sight of the man that had spoken to him in such a kindly and understanding way in the kitchen.

There he was, that solemn pale-faced man with mysterious eyes, whose words had been strong and wise and comforting, like those of a priest in the confessional. Now he sat with bowed head and drooping shoulders. His hands were clasped beneath his chin, as if in prayer. Incomprehension and exhaustion and uncontainable pain were depicted on his countenance, that looked ghostly in the candlelight.

Then pity for this man, whose suffering was manifestly greater than his own, smote the lad's heart and beat upon the wall of bitterness behind which he had taken refuge from advancing terror. He remembered how this man had confessed in the kitchen to having been tempted by a shame similar to his own. He loved Kinsella at that moment, in the way he loved his mother and in the way he had loved the Idea of insurrection, as a means of escape, through faith and discipline, from the prolonged horror of life in the slums; from hunger and loneliness and humiliation. Indeed, as he sat there trembling, with a lump in his throat, the beauty of the Idea again fired his soul with a passionate desire to continue the struggle in spite of terror, like a wild bird, whose shrill voice cries out defiance, as it flies high in a gale over the thundering sea.

Then two shells burst, one after the other, in the building to the south. One of them tore a hole in the southern wall of the restaurant at its eastern end. There was a prolonged rumble of falling masonry. Fragments of burning debris were hurled into the eastern end of the room by the explosion. Like torches, they passed their flames to the tables and the floor. Billowing clouds of acrid smoke also entered. The roar of the fire to the south now became smooth and sustained, like a great wind rushing through a narrow gorge.

The delayed terror now struck the lad in all its might. The great weight that pressed against the pit of his stomach forced out all idea of continuing the struggle. Gasping for breath, he got to his feet and plunged headlong through the hole.

"Come on, lads," shouted the officer with the birdlike face, as he came running from the alcove, "we're getting out of here. Collect all arms and equipment. Look sharp."

Madden was examining the mechanism of the American pistol when he heard the officer's order. His expression of childish delight and abstraction immediately gave place to one of jubilant ferocity. He thrust the pistol into its holster and shook Stapleton.

173

"Come on, comrade," he cried. "Get up."

Stapleton opened his eyes and smiled.

"Excuse me," he said. "I must have fallen asleep."

Men were already running to and fro through the blinding smoke, shouting at the top of their voices, as they searched for their kit.

"Cripes!" Madden said, as he again shook Stapleton violently. "Get on your feet. Didn't you hear the man shout? We're getting out of here in a big hurry. The place is on fire."

Stapleton tried to rise, failed to move his limbs and said, still smiling amiably:

"I'm awfully sorry, but I don't seem able to . . . "

Kinsella approached at that moment, coughing out the acrid smoke that now filled the room. He was staggering. He was no longer able to carry himself with the exaggerated rigidity of a dignified drunkard. His shoulders and his head hung down lifelessly.

"Where is Colgan?" he asked in a thick voice.

"This man has gone dead on us again, sir," Madden said.

"Quite true, Michael," said Stapleton. "I'm so sorry but — "

"What has happened to Colgan?" Kinsella interrupted in a tone of irritation. "Where is he?"

Madden glanced to his left and said:

"Blood'n'ounds! He was sitting there by the wall. The little bastard must have taken to his heels."

Then he picked up his rifle, slung it over his shoulder and took Stapleton in his arms. He had now completely forgotten the promise he made to the little woman. In the strange world that he inhabited with his Idea, the past did not exist.

174

"What about the grub?" he said, as he touched the sack with his foot.

"Leave it," said Kinsella. "We have to cross O'Connell Street and . . ."

Another shell burst against the southern wall at its eastern end, almost in the same position as the previous one. There was a rending sound like a giant piece of cloth being torn. The eastern end of the room became a mass of flames and smoke.

"Come on, lads," shouted the officer with the birdlike face, as he herded his men through the hole in the northern wall. "Get a move on."

Kinsella and his two comrades groped their way to the stairhead.

"It's awfully kind of you, Madden," said Stapleton, as he lay like a baby in Madden's arms. "I feel terribly ashamed of . . ."

"Never mind now," Madden shouted, as he followed Kinsella downstairs. "I could carry a little creature like yourself from Athenry to Ballinrobe. Sure, there's no weight at all in you."

The three men made their way to the front door of the building. There they found three other fugitives, engaged in breaking open the locked door with a pair of crowbars. When the door was broken, these other fugitives plunged onto the pavement and headed straight across O'Connell Street at full speed, under heavy fire from machine guns posted on the south bank of the river. One of them fell on reaching the far pavement.

"You go ahead with George," Kinsella said to Madden. "Make for the Metropole Hotel and run as fast as you can. Keep your head down. I'll follow you."

175

Madden looked at his captain anxiously and said:

"Hadn't we better stay together, sir? You're not . . ."

"Do what I tell you, Madden," Kinsella said sharply.

"Yes, sir," Madden said.

He bowed his head, went through the door and ran across the street, stooping low, towards the northwest. Kinsella followed at a slow walk, with his shoulders and his head drooping, like a man wrapped in thought. He had to grit his teeth in order to urge himself forward. His chest and his sides hurt terribly, as a result of being buried under the falling masonry in the hallway.

Two cavalry horses, that had lost their riders during the charge on Monday and had since been wandering about the neighboring streets without food or water, galloped past the Nelson Pillar towards the south, with their reins trailing and their saddle leathers flapping against their shrunken bellies. They kept neighing in terror, as they ran neck to neck. As they passed Kinsella, one of them received a flesh wound from a bullet in the upper part of the right thigh. The animal swerved sharply and struck Kinsella in the back. He fell forward on his face and lay motionless.

Madden dropped Stapleton in the doorway of the Metropole Hotel. Looking back, he saw that Kinsella had fallen. He ran to his captain, dropped down and asked in a tremulous voice, that had again become thin and high-pitched, what had happened.

"I'm all right," Kinsella muttered.

"Thank God," Madden said fervently.

Then he picked up Kinsella in his arms and carried him across the street.

176

18

ⅅⅅⅅⅅⅅⅅⅅⅅⅅⅅⅅⅅⅅⅅⅅⅅ

THE IMPERIAL TROOPS crossed the river far to the west during the night and then swung eastwards in a wide circle to surround the insurgents' headquarters at the General Post Office. A small party of them, led by a sergeant, came to Mrs. Colgan's house at half past eight next morning, as a result of information received from a group of her neighbors.

"She and her son are both notorious rebels," these neighbors had said to the soldiers. "They have bombs and dynamite in the house."

The sergeant banged on the door with the butt end of his rifle and shouted:

"Open in the King's name."

A large crowd, that included men, women and children, pressed close behind the soldiers, shouting gross insults at the little woman and threatening her life.

"Take her out and hang her from a lamppost," they said to the soldiers with ferocious enthusiasm. "The dirty bitch and her son have brought disgrace and misery down on top of us."

There was really nothing personal in their momentary hatred of Mrs. Colgan. They were afraid of the invading soldiers and offered them the little woman as a sacrifice, hoping it might avert their wrath. Even while they shouted,

177

their faces looked tortured more by shame of what they were doing than by genuine anger.

Mrs. Colgan was roused by the tumult from a profound sleep, which had lasted since eleven o'clock on the previous night, when she threw herself down on her bed without undressing. It was the first sleep she had had since Sunday morning. She spent Sunday night waiting anxiously outside Liberty Hall, where her son was mobilized for the rising with the other members of the Citizen Army. Since parting with Tommy in North Earl Street on Monday night, she had either wandered about the streets trying to get news of him, or else prayed for his safety in her parish church. Then exhaustion finally got the better of her anxiety and she lay down on her bed to sleep.

"Mother of God!" she whispered in fright, as she opened her eyes and listened to the disturbance. "What has happened?"

Her first thought was that the neighbors had come to her with news of her son. Then she became aware that the man calling on her to open the door "in the King's name" did not have an Irish accent and her heart missed a beat.

"It's the soldiers," she gasped. "Ah! Mother of God! It must be all over and my Tommy is either killed or taken."

She made the sign of the cross and pushed aside the quilt that she had drawn over her loins. Then she swung her legs to the floor. At that moment, a shell burst in O'Connell Street to the southwest. The violent explosion would have frightened her under ordinary circumstances. Now it gave her hope and comfort.

"They are still blasting, 'faith," she said to herself, as she moved on tiptoe to the window, "so our lads must be still on their feet, God bless them. My Tommy is not taken yet.

178

If he isn't, though, why should the soldiers be here? How would they know where to come?"

It was only when she peered cautiously from behind the curtain into the street and saw a crowd of her neighbors with the knocking soldiers that she became conscious of the lewd insults and the threats against her life. For a moment or two, she was overwhelmed by the realization that these good people had suddenly turned against her in such a gross and cowardly fashion. She had lived among them for more than sixteen years, without ever once experiencing anything but Irish kindness and true Christian charity at their hands, until this terrible moment. Now they were calling for her blood, as if the devil had suddenly taken possession of them.

"Come on," the sergeant yelled, banging again on the door. "Open up in the King's name and be quick about it."

A short stout man, with a rosy face and curly black hair, pushed his way to the front of the crowd and shouted at the sergeant:

"Yerrah! Don't waste your time. Break down the bloody door and get done with it; or else stand aside and let us deal with her."

The sergeant turned his head abruptly and stared at the rosy-faced man in a hostile and contemptuous fashion.

"Keep back there, you," he said through his clenched teeth.

The rosy-faced man said something under his breath and a craven expression came into his eyes. He stepped to the rear hurriedly.

"What's more," the sergeant continued, as he pointed the muzzle of his rifle at the rosy-faced man, "I advise you to keep your bloody mouth shut, if you know what's good

179

for you. As far as I'm concerned, all you bastards are in the one boat. You are all a pack of rebels."

Mrs. Colgan was infuriated by the remarks of the rosy-faced man. He owned the little grocery shop at the corner. He had always been most friendly with her, often going out of his way to do her a favor. Not only that, but he had on many occasions taken her aside into privacy and confessed in secretive tones that he himself would be in the insurrectionary movement like her son were it not for the fact that he was the father of six young children.

"Jack Finnerty of all people!" she muttered. "Who'd believe it? Ha! It's true for the old saying. Never trust a man that's too polite. Neither can you trust a huckster. He'd sell his country, or his own mother, for a halfpenny profit, just as easily as he'd sell an ounce of tea. He would, 'faith. He'd sell his immortal soul by the ounce. Jack Finnerty! The sniveling hypocrite! It's a wonder the earth doesn't open up and swallow the traitor."

Tears of rage came into her eyes and she thrust forward her hand to draw aside the curtain, raise the window and tell Finnerty what she thought of him. She wanted to tell the others, too, that it would be fitter for them to hand over to the soldiers the goods they had looted than to be felon-setting an honest woman, whose only crime was being the mother of a patriot son.

Instead of acting on that foolish impulse, however, the shrewd little creature withdrew her hand and set her lips resolutely. A cunning expression came into her narrowed eyes behind the tears of rage as she went on tiptoe into the kitchen. There she picked up her hat, her shawl and a small bundle of food from the settle-bed. It was to fetch the bundle of food, intended for her son and Bartly Madden, that she had returned to her home on the previous

180

night. She had been on the point of leaving the house with it when overcome by exhaustion.

"For the last time," she heard the sergeant shout, as she went on tiptoe to the back door, with these articles in her arms, "I order you to open in the King's name."

She drew the bolt of the back door softly and opened it. Then she stepped out into the little yard.

"All right, men," the sergeant cried to his fellows. "Give it a good shoulder. All together now. Shove."

She closed the back door and began to run across the yard just as the front door collapsed. The soldiers rushed into the kitchen as she passed from the yard into a narrow winding lane that led to the southeast. She pulled up the skirt of her white smock and ran as hard as she could down the lane, without waiting to put on her hat and shawl. She turned due east at the end of the lane and went through a short street that opened onto a small square, a short distance to the rear of Moore Street. She halted abruptly as she was about to enter the square, on catching sight of four soldiers who were searching two young men in civilian clothes, about ten yards away to her left. She flattened herself against the wall of a dairy shop and peered cautiously at them from around the corner.

The square was small and oblong, with irregular sides that were pierced by the mouths of five streets, all varying in width. Most of the houses were very old, with broken roofs and sagging walls. None of them was more than two stories in height. The ground was paved with cobblestones, between which dried horse dung and wisps of hay lay ensconced. The two young civilians stood with their backs to a cement horse trough that lay in the center of the square. They held their hands above their heads. Their

181

faces were pale and thin. Their bodies were dwarfed and ill-nourished. Their shabby clothes were torn. Both wore gray tweed caps and colored neck scarves. They stared straight ahead, swaying slightly back and forth, owing to the tension of their posture. Their features expressed no emotion. The four young soldiers were all very young. Their full cheeks were bronzed. Their strong bodies looked well-nourished. Their yellow uniform suits were new. Their tense faces bore a mixed expression of hatred and fear. Three of them were pointing their bayoneted rifles at the two civilians, whom the fourth was searching. None of them spoke. A large number of gaunt and ragged people, some of them fresh from their beds, half-naked and with tousled hair, leaned from windows and doorways all round the square. They watched the scene in dead silence. Their faces also expressd no emotion and they seemed joined in spirit, by some strange passion halted at its height, both with the soldiers and with the young men that were being searched.

A short distance to the east, shells were exploding steadily in the O'Connell Street area. There, too, machine guns and rifles were in violent action and great clouds of smoke rose high into the air from the fires, whose murmur sounded like a broken wave tumbling along a sandy shore, romantic and forlorn. This fierce tumult of battle in the background was like macabre music that gave meaning to the scene enacted in the silent square, where gaunt and ragged people stared from their crumbling houses at their young men being searched by alien soldiers, who carried bayoneted rifles and wore uniform yellow suits; a scene that symbolized the endless cruel tale of invasion and conquest.

After watching for a few moments, Mrs. Colgan put on her shawl and her little round black hat that had a perpendicular white feather stuck in its rear. Seeing that the soldiers had their backs turned towards her and were intent on their chore, she decided that she could escape unnoticed along the side of the square to the right. Thereupon she crept from the wall and trotted cautiously in that direction. She had just entered the mouth of a street that branched off the square to the southwest when an insurgent sniper fired at the soldiers from the roof of a tall building to the east. The bullet found its mark. As she glanced back hurriedly over her shoulder, she saw one of the young soldiers drop his rifle and fall down on his face, with his left hand to his side. She took to her heels as fast as she could. Behind her, the strange silence in the little square was now broken by the sound of running feet and shouting and rifle fire.

She made two further attempts to make her way eastwards by moving to the south, but without any success. The approaches to O'Connell Street were all blocked in that direction, by imperial soldiers that stood in position all the way down to the river. The ring around insurgent headquarters was already tightly closed in that sector. So she turned about and headed due north through a wide street. There she saw imperial flags flying from many windows. Like the inhabitants of her own street, these slum dwellers were trying to curry favor with the invaders by a show of loyalty to the Empire. The very same people that had sung "God Save Ireland" with such fervor on Monday night, as they made carnival with their loot, were now singing marching songs of the imperial soldiers with equal enthusiasm. On all sides, as she passed, she heard people

183

shout insults at the insurgents and pray God for their speedy capture.

"They must all be hanged," she heard the people say. "They are mad dogs. They must be put to death, every mother's son of them."

Resolutely intent on reaching her son, the little creature was undaunted by their hostility. It was only the troops that she feared and she searched the street ahead anxiously for their presence as she advanced. Suddenly she saw a party of them approach, coming round a bend in the road from the west, as she was passing a news vendor's shop. The owner of the shop, a man called Phil Maloney, was known to her. So she opened the door and entered, in order to let the soldiers pass.

"God save all here," she said, closing the door after her.

Phil Maloney and his wife were standing behind the counter. They both looked very tense and just nodded in answer to her salutation. Maloney was a gray-haired old man, with stooping shoulders and a hollow chest. He had once been an active member of the Fenian Brotherhood and had spent over fifteen years in jail. His little shop had acted as a meeting place for the organizations that planned the rising. He and his wife were childless, but they had a nephew out fighting with the Irish Volunteers.

"Have ye any news of Brian?" Mrs. Colgan said to them.

Maloney shook his head. His wife put a handkerchief to her eyes, which were red from weeping.

"Ah! God help ye," Mrs. Colgan said. "Ye are as badly off as myself. It's terrible the way the people have turned against us. My neighbors brought the soldiers to my house. I just managed to get out by the back door. It's hard to believe that Christian Irish people would do such a thing. They did, though."

184

"We expect them here any minute now," Maloney said gloomily.

"Ah! God help you, Mary Anne," his wife said. "What are you going to do now? Have you any place to lay your head?"

"I have no time to think about that now," said the little woman, drawing her shawl close about her. "I must get to my Tommy."

"You had better stay here with us," Mrs. Maloney said. "You are heartily welcome in God's name."

The tramp of marching feet now became loud in the street outside and there was full-throated singing:

If the sergeant drinks your rum, never mind.
He's entitled to his tot, but if he drinks the bloody lot,
The blighter should be shot, so never mind . . .

Maloney went to the window and peered out into the street at the passing column of soldiers. They were all men of mature years, called up from retirement by the government to help deal with the insurrection. They marched with the beautiful precision of old regulars. Their features and their carriage expressed pride in their profession, the renewal of whose practice had been granted to them for a brief moment by an accident of history. Nearly all of them belonged to the neighborhood. A large crowd of women and children trotted along on either side of the column, calling to them by name and cheering and offering gifts.

"It's sad, sure enough," Maloney said in his somber voice, "to see these fighting men of our race go out against those that are trying to give them the dignity of freedom."

"I wouldn't mind these old soldiers so much," said his wife. "It's the people that sicken me. Rich and poor, they are all alike, fawning on their enemies that despise them

185

for their cowardice. What sort of a race are we at all?"

"Don't say that, Lizzie," cried Mrs. Colgan proudly. "Our people are just as good as any other and better than most. Sure, what has a poor person got in life but hunger and fear? How could I blame others, when I ran out by the back door myself? If we are Christians it's our duty to forgive. Then, maybe, we'll be forgiven ourselves. Are we any worse than those who spat on Our Lord going to Calvary? Are we any worse than those who crucified Him?"

"True for you," Phil Maloney said. "Heroes and saints are always crucified, but they rise again to be worshiped by those that crucified them."

"Well! The soldiers are gone now," Mrs. Colgan said, as she turned to leave the shop. "I must be on my way. I must reach my Tommy somehow."

"You are mad to try and reach O'Connell Street," said Maloney. "The soldiers have surrounded it. You had better stay here with us."

"Ah! No," said Mrs. Colgan, as she opened the door. "The Mother of God will find me a way. She won't fail me. How could she refuse to listen to the prayer of a poor suffering mother? She knows what a mother's suffering means. She suffered worse herself."

After leaving the shop, she trotted northwards until she came to a long street that ran eastwards to the northern end of Upper O'Connell Street. She was about to turn into it when she saw that it was occupied by soldiers all along its length, as far as she could see. Some of the soldiers were resting on the pavements. Others stood on guard. Civilians were going to and fro among them, offering them hot tea and sandwiches and cigarettes. As she stood watch-

186

ing, it occurred to her that she might be able to gain passage to the east through this street by pretending to be an imperial supporter and offering the contents of her bundle to the soldiers. She was about to act on this impulse when she became aware of two men who were talking in low voices a few feet away from her, just around the corner. She cocked her ears and listened to what they were saying.

"Yerrah! Not at all," one of the men said. "They are not going to attack the General Post Office today. They won't attack it tomorrow, either. Why lose more men? They've lost enough already, charging foolishly at the point of the bayonet, like the mad Spaniard in the story book. These lads on the north side will draw the ring closer about the Post Office, while the artillery men on the south side push the rebels back into it from their outposts."

"I see what you mean," said the second man. "Like throwing stones at cattle to herd them into a pen."

"You save lives that way," said the first man, "and you don't run the risk of having the ringleaders escape, as might happen in the confusion of a charge."

"There must be a charge, though, sooner or later," said the second man.

"Yerrah! Not at all," said the first man. "There won't be any charge. You wait and see. The rebels will walk through the gap and go into the fold of their own accord, like sheep trying to escape from dogs that are snapping at their heels."

As they both began to laugh softly in their throats, Mrs. Colgan peered cautiously around the corner. She started as she caught sight of the two men. They were both of great size and they were dressed exactly alike, in stout black shoes, blue serge trousers, long fawn raincoats of rough

187

texture and soft brown velours hats, whose brims were drawn far down over their little pig eyes. They stood erect and motionless, with their hands in the pockets of their raincoats, staring straight in front of them. Their profession was obvious to her at a glance.

"G-men!" she muttered in fear.

The presence of these two secret policemen with the soldiers, out in the open for everyone to see, gave her clearly to understand that the defeat of the insurgents was near; far more than their confident words had done. These most detested servants of the government had striven hard to hide themselves from the people since Monday. On Tuesday morning, she had seen one of them dragged from a house by a group of workers and brought into a lane, where he was knocked down and savagely beaten. He whined like a dog, begging for mercy, as he lay on the ground. He would have been kicked to death had not she herself and some other women intervened.

Now these big fellows stood arrogantly behind the advancing soldiers, like well-trained setter dogs waiting patiently at a hunter's heels for the order to go into the covert and "spot" the game. They would receive that order when the rebels had walked "through the gap into the fold." Then they would go in among the captives and identify the important ones with their little pig eyes. Afterwards, it would be their turn to knock down and kick. Neither would there be anybody to intervene, through motives of pity, while they were using their stout black boots on their helpless victims.

She crept away from the corner, ran a little way to the west and then turned north again. She was now praying in silence, trying to conquer the doubts that had assailed her mind for the first time since parting with her son. Then she thought of Madden and her confidence was restored.

"Arrah! What's the matter with me, at all?" she cried aloud as she trotted northwards as fast as she could. "Bartly will look after him. He'll bring my little one back safe to me. Why wouldn't he? Didn't the Blessed Virgin send him across my path? Didn't the Mother of God herself send him to protect my son? Ah! You darling Bartly! I was mad to forget that you are watching over my Tommy."

Spurred by her renewed confidence, she traveled through the northern suburbs right across to the eastern end of the city, turning south now and again, in a vain attempt to find a passage through the ring of soldiers. Alas! There was no hole anywhere through which she could sneak. Up here in the north, the more prosperous citizens were even more hostile to the insurgents than those in the slums. They feasted the soldiers royally. She saw a group of well-dressed women serve roast chicken and wine and cigars to the officers of a battalion that was halted at a crossroads. As she began to become exhausted by her efforts, this hostility of the people finally began to frighten her, even more than the terrible explosions to the south and the immense cloud of smoke that rose into the sky down there. So she abandoned the struggle and turned back. It was then three o'clock in the afternoon.

Weak with hunger and her march, she went into a little restaurant and bought a cup of tea. Then she decided to eat some of the food in her bundle. After having done so, her spirits rose again.

"I'll go and ask the Blessed Virgin to help me," she said to herself.

She left the restaurant and hurried to her parish church.

There she went on her knees before the little altar of the Blessed Virgin. After she had prayed for a little while, it seemed to her that another miracle had been performed on her behalf; for she thought of a plan that would enable her to break through the ring of soldiers and reach O'Connell Street without hindrance.

"Mother of God!" she whispered with fervor, while tears rolled down her cheeks. "I thank you from the bottom of my heart."

She stayed in the church until the fall of night. Then she made her way back to the corner where she had stood that morning, watching the four soldiers search the two civilians by the horse trough in the little square. She halted there and prayed for a little while. Then she pushed her hat to the back of her head, drew her hair down in disorder about her cheeks, took off her shawl and held it down by her right side, with one end trailing along the ground. She held her little bundle of food in her left hand. Finally she twisted her face into a drunken grimace and looked around the corner.

The square was now in darkness, except for rivulets of light that flowed from open doorways and through window curtains at its eastern end. Soldiers were walking to and fro over there. The heavy tread of their boots on the pavement sounded mysterious and subdued. Their indistinct bodies looked ghoulish and menacing, like those of animals on the prowl. Now and again, one of them came out of the shadows and passed through a stream of light into an open doorway to become engaged with a woman that was waiting there. Couples became silhouetted for a moment against the drawn curtains of windows on the upper floors. Sudden low cries and ripples of laughter came

190

from these upper rooms at irregular intervals; like sounds of unseen life heard at night in a forest.

"Well! Here goes in God's name," the little woman said to herself.

Then she staggered out into the square and headed due east, trailing her shawl along the ground and jabbering unintelligibly. Now and again, she raised a shout and waved her bundle above her head.

"Hey! You drunken old cow!" a soldier said to her, as she reached the eastern end. "Put a sock in it."

She halted, looked at the man, swayed from side to side twice, waved her bundle above her head and broke into song:

Oh! I was born in Boston, a city you all know well,
Brought up by honest parents, the truth . . .

Another soldier came up behind her, prodded her in the rump with the butt end of his rifle and said in a jovial tone:

"Run along now, granny. You should be jolly well ashamed of yourself for getting blotto at your age."

She turned and stared at the man, with her teeth bared in a foolish grin. Then she stuck out her tongue and made a vulgar sound with her lips, like a naughty and ill-mannered child.

"That for you, my man," she said.

"Get out of here," said the soldier, "before I lose my temper with you. Go on home to your Paddy."

Mrs. Colgan lurched sideways, as she tried to swing her bundle over her head in a belligerent gesture.

"Don't you threaten me," she cried, "or it might be the worse for you. I could lick six men of your size."

191

Several soldiers began to laugh.

"Aw! Don't hurt us, granny," one of them said. "There's a dear."

"All right, then," she said, "but keep a civil tongue in your heads."

She did a little caper and then staggered forward towards the mouth of an alleyway that led into Moore Street, singing in a cracked voice:

> *Oh! The Russians and the Yankees*
> *Their hearts were full of glee . . .*

"Hey! Where do you think you're going?" cried a soldier, as she entered the alleyway. "You might get a packet in the napper down there."

Paying no heed to the man, she staggered onwards singing:

> *For they were sure their bully boy*
> *Would kill John Morrissey. . . .*

The big guns had now finished with the eastern side of Lower O'Connell Street, which was all in flames. They were trying to find the range of the General Post Office. A shell that had overreached its mark burst at that moment near the horse trough in the little square. The soldiers dropped to the ground. A chorus of shrill cries came from the crumbling houses.

The little woman hurriedly abandoned her role of drunkard and fled headlong to the end of the lane. There she began to knock on the side door of a butcher's shop that fronted Moore Street.

"Thank you," she said to the Blessed Virgin as she knocked. "Thank you kindly."

19

JUUUUUUUUUUUUUUUUUUUUUUL

IT WAS NOW FRIDAY MORNING shortly after
dawn in a corner bedroom on an upper floor of the Metropole Hotel. Kinsella lay asleep on the bed, with his left
forearm across his eyes and his right knee bent. He shuddered spasmodically and made a little whining sound in
his throat, like a dog dreaming of the chase. His right
foot kept jerking sideways, as if he were trying to rid himself of some annoyance. Madden slept on the floor by the
rear wall. He lay motionless on his back with an eiderdown
quilt spread across his middle and a pillow under his head.
His fingers were laced on his chest. He was breathing softly
like a child. Stapleton was wide awake. He sat astride a
chair before the window that faced Lower O'Connell
Street. His chin rested on his hands, which were crossed
over the back of the chair. He was peering over the barricade at the great fires that raged across the street, all the
way from the Nelson Pillar to the bridge. His lips were
parted and his brilliant blue eyes looked awed by the
majesty of the spectacle.

The air in the room was still faintly charged with the
perfume used by the woman that was living there when the
insurgents came to take possession of the hotel. She had
left in great haste without taking her belongings. Her black

silk nightdress lay on the back of an armchair and her toilet articles were scattered over the dressing table. A pair of dainty red slippers stood on the floor by the wardrobe. The door was wide open. Men were running to and fro in the corridor to the left, shouting excitedly. Rifle and machine gun bullets thudded against the outer walls of the room. The somber gray bulk of the General Post Office was visible through the side window that faced north. It was only a few yards away, on the far side of Prince's Street. Shells were exploding at intervals against its roof. Other shells burst overhead in the hotel whose topmost floors had already been partially destroyed.

The crash of the exploding shells and the harsh rattle of the smaller arms sounded trivial compared to the roar of the fires; just as when a forest is being consumed, the snapping of branches and even the resounding fall of giant trees make hardly any impression on the vast tumult of the toiling flames, the murmur of whose breath maintains a constant and unbroken rhythm.

Kinsella suddenly made a gasping sound in his throat, sat up in the bed and looked about him wildly. His gaunt bearded face now wore an expression of horror, like that of a hermit monk grappling with a violent temptation of the flesh.

"What happened?" he said to Stapleton.

Stapleton turned towards him and said gently:

"Were you dreaming, Michael?"

Kinsella swung his legs to the floor, making a grimace owing to the pain that movement caused his hurt body. Then he sat on the edge of the bed and covered his face with his hands for a few moments.

When he again looked at Stapleton, the expression of

194

horror had left his eyes. Now they were terribly sad and uncomprehending.

"Of course, it was a dream," he said calmly. "Even so, I find it strange that I should have a dream, because I don't remember ever having dreamt before; at least, not since I was a child. It's still most painfully vivid in my mind, just as if it had actually happened to me in real life. It's a frightening experience."

"Perhaps it did really happen," said Stapleton.

Kinsella frowned and said:

"What do you mean? How could a dream really happen?"

"We have now reached," said Stapleton, "what the Spaniards call 'la hora de la verdad,' the supreme moment of passion when the whole of life is expressed in a single gesture; when the soul is stripped naked and its real nature is exposed."

"I still don't understand what you mean," said Kinsella. "All that sounds like mysticism."

"Tell me what you dreamed," said Stapleton.

Kinsella stared at the floor, clasped his hands between his thighs and said in a low voice:

"I stood in an immense valley, on the bank of a narrow river that flowed through a chasm of great depth. Behind me, the valley was studded with the ruins of cities and villages. There was no sign of life back there. The earth was barren. All was silent and mournful, as if the world had come to an end. Out in front, beyond the river, lay one city that was whole and of great beauty. The people going to and fro in the streets were godly in appearance and their faces were radiant with happiness. I could hear their laughter and the sound of exquisite music came to me

195

from unseen instruments. Before the city, just beyond a bridge that spanned the river, a most extraordinary flower grew from a large golden urn, that stood at the center of a platform on an eminence. It had a black stem and scarlet petals. The stem grew rapidly, until its head stood far above the roofs of the houses. Then it cast its petals in an overarching shower and disappeared, only to begin growing again at once from the urn, with the same rapidity. It kept rising up continually to its great height and showering its petals on the people, who caught them as they fell and smelled their perfume. A group of young girls, all dressed in white, danced around the urn. They sang and threw incense from golden thuribles at the flower as they danced. I tried desperately to cross the bridge and enter the city, in order to catch one of the petals and smell its perfume, but I could not do so. A reptile had entwined its body about my legs and I was unable to escape from its embrace. It kept reaching upwards, throwing coil after coil about me, until I finally began to choke."

He shuddered, drew the back of his right hand across his eyes and looked at Stapleton.

"It was horrible torture," he added, "not being able to cross the bridge and catch one of the petals, because I was aware that it was their perfume which made the people so happy. It reached me ever so faintly on my side of the bridge, but its quality was drowned in the foul odor of death that filled the air.

"It was really frightful, being aware of such delight and yet being denied it."

Stapleton looked out the window and said:

"How beautiful! I mean the black and scarlet flower, that died when it had reached its fullness, only to be born again at once in all its glory. The slow death of a flower and the long wait of its seed in the earth before rebirth has always seemed to me most cruel. How lovely and gay it looks with summer's warm kiss upon its heart! Then day by day its beauty fades, until the frosty autumn winds tear down its shriveled petals, scatter its seed and leave only the naked stalk drooping in winter's snow, like a battered sign over a forgotten grave."

He turned quickly towards Kinsella once more and said in an excited tone:

"I understand your dream perfectly. The reptile, of course, represents the tragedy that changed the course of your life, preventing you from doing what you were born to do."

Kinsella's face flushed.

"What tragedy?" he said angrily. "You are talking nonsense."

"No, no, Michael," said Stapleton. "It's not nonsense."

"Of course it is," said Kinsella. "You know that I detest mysticism."

"Please, don't get annoyed," said Stapleton, "I'll explain what I mean. As I said just now, this is the hour of truth, when the soul stands naked before its destiny."

"There is no such thing as destiny," said Kinsella, "and a naked soul is a pretty farfetched idea."

"At this hour," Stapleton continued imperturbably, "one feels the exaltation of fulfillment if one has done and is doing what one was born to do. If not, one suffers the agony of despair and the shame of having lived in a lie, of having allowed oneself to be regarded as a hero while one was really a mountebank; for the lie is then mercilessly laid bare."

197

"There was no tragedy in my life," said Kinsella with force.

"Oh yes, Michael," said Stapleton, "there was. You told me so yourself that evening two years ago, when we went walking together on the mountains. It was then that we became friends and I remember every word you said. You didn't tell me exactly what caused you to abandon your studies and become a schoolmaster, but I understood that you suffered terribly by having to do so. You said that your life until then had been a glorious voyage of discovery towards the ever-lengthening horizon of human knowledge. Afterwards it became a sordid round of drudgery without purpose."

"There was no tragedy," said Kinsella with great force. "I may have thought so then, through vanity and selfishness, but I now think differently. I have since learned the truth."

"It was a tragedy," said Stapleton, "and it still is, no matter what you say. Otherwise, you couldn't possibly have dreamed of the reptile that kept you from crossing the bridge and tasting the delights of . . . "

"I tell you that it was vanity," Kinsella interrupted, almost at the top of his voice, "and stop talking nonsense. After all, I am the best judge of what constitutes tragedy in my life."

Then he frowned, looked at the floor and continued in a lower tone:

"By the time I had taken my master's degree, I was convinced that I was about to become one of the world's greatest chemists. I gloated over the flattering things being said about me in scholastic circles. Then my mother died suddenly, just as I was about to go abroad for a post-

198

graduate course. Her annuity expired with her death and I knew that she had set her heart on my brother becoming a priest. He had just entered the Irish College at Rome. I had to give up my traveling scholarship and take a job, so as to enable him to get ordained. He died shortly before I had that conversation with you, as the result of an accident. That was why I spoke so bitterly, finding it unfair that I should have been called upon to make a sacrifice which proved to be unnecessary. Since then, I have learned that no sacrifice is worthless, because it is its own reward. The only thing in life that counts is to do one's duty. Everything else is vanity and foolishness."

"I knew it," said Stapleton. "You tried to kill the poet in you, in an attempt to become a saint; but the poet remains, still wanting to continue that glorious journey towards the horizon of the unknown, where the black and scarlet flower . . ."

"Say what you please, George," Kinsella interrupted. "I know I'm right. If there really is such a thing as your hour of truth, then I had mine last Sunday in my room, when I struggled to overcome . . ."

He stopped speaking suddenly, disturbed by the sounds of Madden's awakening. Then he looked at the Connemara man in an indignant and even hostile manner. Stapleton also looked at Madden in the same way. There was really nothing personal in their attitude of hostility. They were merely annoyed at having a third person break in upon their intimate discussion.

After yawning and stretching his limbs for a little while, Madden sat up against the wall, rolling his tongue from side to side in his mouth and making sour grimaces, like a person that has just tasted something unpleasant. Then he thrust aside the quilt, flexed his biceps, jerked back his shoulders several times, rubbed his eyes and looked about the room, sniffing like a dog that has come into a strange place. His unshaven face, blackened by the grime of battle and deeply lined by fatigue, looked many years older. His fierce blue eyes now had the look of dark wisdom that comes from taking part with ecstasy in the dance of death.

He nodded casually to Stapleton and then put his fingers to the brim of his cap as he addressed Kinsella in a gruff tone.

"Feeling any better, Captain?" he said.

"Much better, thank you," said Kinsella shortly.

Madden scratched his sides with his elbows vigorously for a few moments. Then he threw back his head and yawned at great length.

"Thank God, you had no bones broken in any case," he said, "although you were badly battered. Blood'n'ounds! You're black all over."

Then he leaped smartly to his feet and laughed.

"You're nearly as bad as I was," he cried in a jovial tone, "that night the peelers got at me in Galway's barracks with their boots."

Standing with his legs wide apart, he drew in a deep breath through his nostrils, while raising his arms slowly to their full length above his head. After pausing for a moment with his chest expanded to the limit, he opened his mouth and dropped his arms stiffly to his sides as he expelled the air from his lungs in a violent rush. Then he picked up his rifle, slung it across his back and strode to the window that faced O'Connell Street, swaying jauntily at the hips.

He now wore brown top boots and a heavy fleece-lined

200

waterproof coat of military cut over his blue serge suit. He had found them in a bedroom that had been hurriedly evacuated by an imperial army officer on furlough from the Flanders battle front. They fitted him perfectly and already looked quite in keeping with his bedraggled gray tweed cap. Both the coat and the boots had got torn and scorched in many places while he was helping to put out a fire on the top floor during the early part of the night. He had also added a cloth bandolier, that he took from a wounded man, to his war equipment. Stuffed with rifle ammunition, it was slung across his body, over the shoulder strap of the fine officer's belt that he had taken from the dead man in the kitchen.

Leaning over Stapleton's back, he stared across the street at the fires for a few moments in silence. Then he wagged his head several times in admiration of the scene.

"Blood'n'ounds!" he said. "I never in all my life saw such a blaze. By the hammers of hell! You wouldn't see that much smoke on our whole shore, when the kelp is being burned. Yet I saw nearly two hundred kilns once, all lit at the same time and so near together that their smoke made a wall. That was a fine sight, too, with the men shouting like mad as they worked with their crowbars and a crowd of women singing in the moonlight and jugs of poitín going the rounds. Arrah! It was nothing compared to this, though. There will be ballads written about this blaze here. It's the king of all the fires that ever were."

Then he gripped Stapleton's shoulder in a friendly gesture, turned about and strode from the room.

"I'll look for some tea," he said, going out the door.

Stapleton sighed with relief as he watched Madden disappear into the corridor. Then he turned to Kinsella.

"How odd that is," he whispered. "I was afraid of that man just now, while he was bending over me, just as if he were a primeval creature, utterly remote from my consciousness and unpredictable."

"I understand what you mean," said Kinsella. "I had that very same feeling as I watched him rise from the floor and stretch himself with the sensual pleasure of an awakening animal."

"Yet I'm really very fond of him," said Stapleton. "He carried me in his arms and was awfully kind to me. Why should I fear him? He is so gentle and innocent, in spite of his fierce nature."

"He is no longer innocent," said Kinsella. "That is the trouble. When I saw him first, I knew instinctively that he wanted to join us simply for the love of fighting and not because he felt that it was his duty. Yet he looked so sincere that I let him come. Now that he has drawn blood, though, the evil in his nature has come to the surface. I blame myself for what has happened to him. Since we left the outpost, I've been so tired that I lost control over him. Left to his own resources . . ."

"Don't worry about him, Michael," Stapleton interrupted. "He's all right. In fact, I envy him. Weep not for him, but for yourself and for me. At this hour of truth, he's going to meet his destiny doing what he was born to do. You and I, though, are not soldiers. We hate bloodshed. Yet we are here."

"I disagree profoundly," said Kinsella, in an indignant tone. "We are here, George, because we are doing our duty."

"Not I," said Stapleton. "I loathe that word. My father believes, like you, that fulfillment of one's duty is the supreme virtue. He's doing his duty in France at the moment, defending his empire against the Germans. I disagree with him violently, but I'm not here out of spite, trying to detach this island from his empire. That would be childish and ridiculous. Why put a different gang of charlatans in power here, so that they might make worse laws than the old?"

"Then why are you here?" said Kinsella angrily.

A mocking light came into Stapleton's eyes and he laughed in a peculiar manner, without any merriment.

"Who knows?" he cried in a high-pitched voice, with his head canted to one side. "Perhaps I'm an alley cat and I've come to warm myself at that big fire. Or I might be a foolish little bird that thinks the red light over there is the sun come down to earth. I may be here to sing my last song in praise of this stupendous dawn."

"Stop it, George," Kinsella cried with great force.

"What's wrong with my being a cat or a bird?" Stapleton continued in the same mocking tone. "Be I good or bad, I am a poet and all poets are pantheists like Shelley. At least they should be, for to be a poet is to be supremely capable of love, not as a lustful miser in search of sensual pleasure, but like your black and scarlet flower that showered its divine bounty on all without exception. Surely you will admit that Shelley was one of us. He once threw down pamphlets from his hotel window into this very street outside, urging the people to revolt. Even the most stupid and narrow-minded person will admit that God has created all creatures. He will maintain it with conviction while he is eating one of them with gusto; perhaps a dish of larks' wings, or a dainty morsel of innocent young lamb that has been slaughtered for his pleasure. Of course, the

203

omnivorous brute will also maintain that he himself is the only one of God's creatures made in God's own image and that he alone has an immortal soul. In that I differ with him. I believe that the whole universe is God and that He is equally present in all creatures and in all things, whose existence has absolutely no purpose, other than to serve as an expression of His will to love."

"Stop it, George," Kinsella cried out once more, raising his voice to a shout. "I can't allow you to say such things at this moment."

Two bright spots appeared at the center of Stapleton's hollow cheeks. His expanded nostrils twitched. He threw back his head and stared at Kinsella, with an expression of exalted dignity on his face.

"I'm an insurgent par excellence," he cried in a defiant tone. "I'm in revolt against the whole concept of good and evil current in our age. I'm in revolt against all forms of government, because they are all based on the same false concept of morality. Above all, I'm in revolt against the idea that man is the center of the universe and that he is made in God's image. To me, that is blasphemy and outrageous nonsense. It is the root of all evil."

Kinsella shuddered, bowed his head, put his elbows on his knees and rested his chin on his cupped hands.

"I'm sorry for being angry with you," he said gently. "I'm awfully tired. That's why I'm so irritable."

Stapleton's distraught countenance became composed and he smiled in a most charming manner as he bowed to Kinsella.

"Forgive me, too," he said, "for being pompous."

"We were both pompous," said Kinsella. "We both said silly things."

204

"That's only natural," said Stapleton. "We are both tipsy with an emotion that is too strong for us to contain."

Then he laughed gaily, looked out the window and continued to speak in a casual tone.

"Here's a very peculiar thing, Michael," he said. "Have you noticed that there's been no rain since last Sunday? It must be the first time in history that no rain has fallen on Dublin for five successive days during the month of April. It's just as if the weather were in league with the government. It's certainly been a great help, this drought, in burning us out of our positions. A few good showers might have made all the difference. The flames must really be ardent supporters of the Empire, for they are taking extreme delight in the work. They look exactly like a horde of wicked creatures, as they rush madly from room to room, destroying everything in their path. Just now they are having great sport with some very inflammable material they found in a shop — chemicals, I dare say, or oil. Oh! How beautiful! A sheet of flame is rising to a height of more than fifty feet, through an immense column of fawn-colored smoke. The pillar of fire is all the colors of the rainbow."

Madden entered the room at that moment in a state of great excitement. He halted briefly within the door, looked wildly at Kinsella, opened his mouth to speak and then closed it again without saying anything.

"What is it, Madden?" said Kinsella.

Madden walked slowly to a small table that stood by the head of the bed. There he set down a jug of tea and a plate, on which there were three cups and some buttered bread. Then he looked intently at Kinsella, with bewilderment and suspicion in his eyes.

"Out with it," said Kinsella.

205

"There's talk of surrender," Madden said in a low voice.

Stapleton leaped from his chair and ran over to the bed with surprising agility. Kinsella got to his feet slowly and drew himself to his full height.

"Surrender?" cried Stapleton in a tone of horror. "Who's talking of surrender?"

"What did you hear, Madden?" Kinsella said quietly.

"There's a crowd of men in a room down there," Madden said, "gathered round a little fellow that has just come from the General Post Office. I heard the little fellow say that the leaders are in two minds since General Connolly got wounded yesterday. He said we are surrounded now on all sides and that all our positions are lost, from here down to the river. Our lads beyond the river, he said, are surrounded as well and they can't budge an inch. So it's foolishness, according to him, going on with the fight until we are all massacred. A few of the men were terrified by what he said. They got on their knees and pulled out their rosary beads and began to pray like old women."

"You should have shot him like a dog," cried Stapleton.

"I didn't like to interfere," Madden said, with his suspicious eyes still fixed on Kinsella, "on account of what you told me the other day, after I struck that man."

"Where is this room, Madden?" said Kinsella.

"Three doors down on the left," Madden said.

Kinsella drew his pistol as he walked stiffly to the door.

"May I come with you, Michael?" said Stapleton.

"Stay there, both of you," said Kinsella. "Have some breakfast. I may be gone some time."

Madden sat down on the bed after Kinsella had gone. He poured a cup of tea from the jug and drank some. Then

206

he began to eat a slice of bread, with his eyes fixed on the far wall.

"It's ridiculous," said Stapleton, as he searched the pockets of his uniform. "I find myself without a weapon of any sort. What on earth happened to the rifle that I had?"

He went back to his chair, sat down and listened intently, with his head canted sideways, to the disorderly chorus of sound. He remained motionless for a few minutes, listening that way. Then he started and looked at Madden.

"Did you hear anything?" he said.

Madden swallowed what he had in his mouth, scowled and said:

"What would I hear?"

Then he took another piece of bread from the plate and began to eat it.

"It's not what one does in life that counts," said Stapleton, "but how one does it. The slightest gesture may be a dance of great beauty, while the most ambitious and noble undertaking loses all merit by a lack of dignity."

He brought his chair over to the bed, sat down and poured a cup of tea from the jug. As he sipped the tea, he watched Madden's face intently.

"You mustn't lose faith in Michael," he said suddenly in a low voice.

Madden started and continued to stare at the far wall for a few moments. Then he turned his head slowly and glared at Stapleton.

"What do you mean?" he growled.

He knew very well what Stapleton meant, because his faith in Kinsella had been shaken by what he heard in the other room. The doubts that now assailed him were far different from those he experienced during the battle at the bridge. For the first time since Monday night, when he accepted Kinsella as his leader with his whole heart and soul, the Idea itself was in danger of being overwhelmed.

"Don't be afraid," said Stapleton earnestly, as he took a piece of bread from the plate. "No matter what happens, Michael is not going to surrender. Neither will I, for that matter, but it's on Michael that you rely. It doesn't really matter to you what I do."

"I don't know what you're talking about," Madden said in a menacing tone. "I wouldn't say any more, if I were you."

"That's quite all right," said Stapleton. "There's nothing more unpleasant than to have somebody peep into one's conscience. I merely want to tell you that a moment will come, before the end, when you'll have to stand alone, without any support other than your faith."

"Shut up," Madden shouted.

Kinsella returned to the room twenty minutes later. Watched intently by Madden and Stapleton, he came over to the bed. His face showed no emotion, but his carriage was now buoyant, as if his body were no longer in pain. He sat down on the side of the bed, looked at Madden and smiled.

"Any tea left?" he said in a tone of suppressed excitement.

Madden started on detecting the changed tone of his captain's voice. Then a faint tremor passed down his spine and his face became radiant, just as when Kinsella had first spoken to him in North Earl Street on Monday night. The Idea again took triumphant possession of him. He

208

jumped to his feet and took the jug from the table with a trembling hand.

"It's cold now, Captain," he said hoarsely. "I'll go and look for some more."

Down the corridor, men began to sing "The Soldiers' Song." Others were cheering wildly.

"Never mind," said Kinsella, putting a hand on Madden's arm. "It doesn't matter about its being cold. Give me a cup."

Madden's hand now trembled so much that he spilled a little of the tea as he filled the cup.

"You have news, Michael," Stapleton whispered eagerly. "What is it?"

Kinsella drank the whole contents of the cup at one draught. Then he leaned back and smiled.

"An order has just come from headquarters," he said. "All available men are to muster this evening at the General Post Office, for an attempt to break through the enemy lines after dark towards the northwest and join forces with our comrades in the provinces."

"Oh!" said Stapleton in a tone of relief. "That's good. I was afraid for a moment . . . "

Images of seen beauty passed through Madden's mind as he stood with his lips parted and his head thrown back, listening to the shouted song.

20

ЛЛЛЛЛЛЛЛЛЛЛЛЛЛЛЛЛЛЛЛЛЛ

A̶ll through the morning and the early
part of the afternoon, small parties of insurgents reached
the Metropole at intervals from positions farther to the
south on the western side of O'Connell Street. When the
last of these men had arrived, the officer in charge gave
the order to leave the hotel. The whole garrison then
assembled on the ground floor, by the side entrance facing
Prince's Street. They had to wait there for some time, while
a large party of women left the General Post Office and
passed westwards through Prince's Street.

The women carried out their movement in great disorder. Most of them were serving with the insurgent
forces as auxiliaries and wore green uniforms, to which
belts and haversacks were attached. The remainder were
nurses, dressed in white, with red crosses on their bosoms.
They were all in a state bordering on panic as they
emerged from the side door of the General Post Office, as
a result of being subjected for a long time to the horror of
artillery bombardment; an experience that is generally beyond the endurance of their sex. Furthermore, they had
been confined since morning, as a measure of safety, to
the cellars of the building. Sitting underground for so
many hours in enforced idleness, listening to the horrid

noises overhead and expecting the ammunition stored down there to explode at any moment, they had preyed on one another's nerves by gloomy conversation and fits of hysteria. It was only natural, therefore, that they should rush frantically into Prince's Street, entirely beyond control of their own will and the authority of their commander, in their eagerness to escape from a place that had caused them such pain. Alas! The scene outside increased their terror. On either side of the narrow street, the Metropole Hotel and the General Post Office were ablaze in their upper stories. The rumble of falling masonry issued from both buildings. To the east, the far side of O'Connell Street was a wall of flames and smoke. To the west, in the direction they were going, a wooden barricade that stretched across Prince's Street was burning. Finding themselves surrounded on all sides by flames, the hapless creatures kept running back and forth for several minutes, screaming and clutching at one another, now trying to re-enter the building they had just abandoned, then scurrying east to the corner of O'Connell Street and again charging madly to the west, until their commander finally managed to regain control and lead them safely through the barricade; like a flock of migrating birds that set up a violent chatter as they rise from the ground in a long undulating scarf that soars whirling to the upper firmament, where they break into a scattered shower of unrelated bodies that keep changing direction in seeming indecision and then suddenly cohere into a broad-based wedge that rushes in a straight line towards its goal.

The men, waiting in tense silence within the open doorway of the hotel, watched this scene with complete indifference to the suffering of the fleeing women; not through inhumanity, but because they were already united in spirit with their enemies, whom they hoped to meet at last in combat hand to hand, after being cooped up in buildings under bombardment for several days and denied the passion of contact. Indeed, they never heard the cries of terror that came from these weaker creatures, who were being sent to the rear lest they might be an encumbrance during the sortie. They were listening to the battle anthem that their comrades had begun to sing within the General Post Office. As soon as the women had passed, they left the hotel in small groups and marched across the street, silent and orderly, to their crumbling headquarters. There they entered a very large high-ceilinged room, where the whole insurgent force was being assembled for departure.

It was then half-past six o'clock and still broad daylight outside, but the great room was already in semi-darkness owing to the thick mass of smoke that filled the air. Indeed, practically the only light came through a large hole in the roof from the flames in the upper stories of the building. This weird light, filtering through the smoke, intensified the look of exaltation on the faces of the men, who stood singing defiantly by the walls, or knelt on the floor, telling their beads. The voices were audible only at intervals, owing to the thunder of the exploding shells and the rattle of rifle ammunition that had been set on fire in various parts of the building.

Madden was very restless as he took up position with Stapleton by the western wall, near the hole in the roof, while Kinsella went to confer with other officers that were making preparations for the sortie. He had been that way ever since Kinsella returned to the bedroom with news.

212

After cleaning his weapons and setting his gear in proper order with meticulous care, he had wandered about the hotel like a hen looking for a place to lay her egg. To occupy his time, he had shaved himself with a razor that he found, brushed most of the dirt from his waterproof coat and polished his top boots. He looked very spruce as a result. He now examined his weapons once more, counted his ammunition, adjusted his equipment and rummaged in his pockets that were stuffed with various other useful articles he had collected, like a nervous traveler that keeps pulling out his passport and his money and his tickets. At a loss for further employment, he shifted back and forth by the wall, stretching himself and stiffening his muscles. His mind was without coherent thought and he was indifferent to what was happening in the room. The hammer was again beating time against his forehead. His whole being waited with almost unbearable desire for a repetition of the wild ecstasy he had experienced during the fight at the bridge.

After about ten minutes, unable to endure the suspense in silence any longer, he turned to Stapleton and said:

"What's keeping the captain? Why are we waiting here?"

Stapleton did not show any sign of having heard these questions. He was leaning against the wall in a most casual manner, with his left hand in his trouser pocket and his feet crossed. In his right hand, that hung limply by his side, he carried the revolver that Madden had given him before leaving the hotel. Judging by the way he held the weapon, with his forefinger through the trigger guard, he did not attach great importance to its possession. His head was thrown back and his parted lips kept moving, as if forming words. Yet no sound issued from them. His

213

pale emaciated face looked solemn and his eyes were very strained. There were beads of perspiration on his forehead.

"Blood'n'ounds!" Madden said, as he gripped him by the arm and shook him. "Why don't you answer me? Wake up, man."

Stapleton then turned his head slowly and looked at Madden vaguely, as if the man were a stranger to him.

"Had you spoken to me?" he said.

"Cripes!" Madden said. "You must have been asleep with your eyes open. I shouted at you loud enough to wake the dead."

"Not asleep," said Stapleton. "I was recalling pleasant things. There may not be much time left, you know, so that each remaining moment of reverie is extremely precious."

"What sort of talk is that?" Madden growled. "Pull yourself together. Look at the way you're holding that revolver. We may be stepping out of here any minute now. Sure, you couldn't fight your own shadow in that condition. Do you hear me? Wake up, man."

"I would only make you angry by trying to explain," said Stapleton gently. "In any case, I don't want to talk just now. Each man must prepare for the supreme moment in his own way and in absolute solitude."

He turned away, looked into the distance and added: "Please don't be offended. I don't mean to be rude."

Disturbed by these remarks that were incomprehensible to him, Madden moved away a little from his strange companion and began to fuss once more with his gear, in an effort to contain his violent desire for action. It was no use. The hammer in his head quickened the tempo of its striking and his feet began to itch.

"Blast it!" he cried at length, as he looked around the room angrily at the men that were singing and praying. "What's going on here?"

A shell exploded at that moment overhead. Pieces of shrapnel came through the hole in the roof. One of them struck a man who was kneeling in prayer on the floor, a short distance in front of Madden. He screamed and raised his joined hands, about which rosary beads were entwined, high above his head, as if taken by an ecstasy of worship. Then he dropped his hands smartly to his chest and bowed low until his head almost touched the floor. He paused for a moment in that attitude, making a gurgling sound in his throat like water pouring through a narrow funnel. Finally, he turned over on his side and began to kick with his left leg.

Madden was going forward to help the fallen man when he noticed that Stapleton had dropped his revolver and was slipping down against the base of the wall. His fierce countenance immediately became gentle and compassionate. He rushed over and threw himself down beside his comrade.

"Ah! Lord God!" he whispered in a broken voice. "Where are you hurt?"

Stapleton was now sitting against the base of the wall, with his left leg doubled under his rump and his right leg thrust out straight along the floor. He had received a severe wound in the right side above the groin. Although he was still master of the pain and had made no sound since he got hit, he was having great difficulty in controlling his features. They kept breaking into spasmodic movement, like the undulating surface of liquid that has just reached boiling point. The expression of

215

his eyes had changed in an extraordinary fashion. Ordinarily wide-open and brilliant, as if enraptured by the beauty of the world, their compass had narrowed and advancing fear had made them sharp.

He managed to smile faintly as he answered Madden in a low tone.

"Excuse me," he said, "but my left leg is bent under me. Could you straighten it?"

He bared his clenched teeth as Madden half-lifted him in order to straighten the leg. His whole face was now perspiring freely.

"Where is the wound?" Madden said.

"In my side," said Stapleton. "Where is Michael? I want to see him."

"He'll be here any moment now," Madden said hurriedly, as he took a packet of field dressing from his pocket. "Take it easy, comrade. I'll fix up your cut in no time at all."

"No, no," Stapleton protested with all his remaining strength, as Madden went to unbutton his tunic. "Please don't touch me."

Madden paused and said in a comforting tone:

"Don't be afraid, lad. I won't hurt you. I'm a great hand with cuts. At home, I was always in great demand when cattle were . . ."

"No, no," Stapleton insisted. "It's not that. I want to remain properly dressed. Please don't touch me."

"All right then," Madden said. "It's so dark here now, in any case, that it would be hard to do a good job on it. I'd better carry you out of here to some place . . ."

"No, no," Stapleton cried in a shrill tone. "Don't move me. Don't you understand that I'm dying?"

216

"Dying?" Madden whispered hoarsely, as he peered closely at Stapleton's face, which was now in manifest agony. "You poor man, is it that bad?"

Exhausted by the violent effort he had made to defend his person, Stapleton now had great difficulty in keeping his back to the wall. His head was drooping down over his chest.

"Yes, yes," he whispered. "I'm dying. That's quite all right, though."

"Is there nothing at all I can do for you?" Madden said.

"Find Michael," said Stapleton. "Find him quickly because . . ."

"All right, comrade," Madden said as he got to his feet.

A number of men entered the far side of the room at that moment and began to shout in urgent tones:

"Come on, lads, get a move on. Pack it up. Get out of here."

The singing changed into a wild cheer, in which those who had been praying on their knees took part. When all were on their feet and moving towards the door, the song burst forth again in a mighty roar:

Soldiers are we whose lives are pledged to Ireland
Some have come from a land . . .

Madden had begun to push his way across the floor through the press of singing men when he saw Kinsella approach.

"Hurry, Captain," he shouted. "Stapleton got hit."

Then he rushed back to find that Stapleton had fallen over on his side and was making futile efforts to resume a sitting position.

"Take it easy, now, comrade," he said.

"It mustn't be lying down," Stapleton whispered urgently, as Madden stooped over him. "Put me against the wall. Lift me."

"All right, comrade," Madden said.

Stapleton seemed to have now passed beyond pain, because he gave no sign of suffering when Madden lifted him. His breathing had become very loud and hoarse.

"Where is Michael?" he gasped, when he was again propped against the wall. "Did you find him?"

"He's coming," Madden said.

"Where is he?" Stapleton said. "Tell him to hurry."

Kinsella arrived at that moment and went on his knees beside his stricken friend.

"Here I am, George," he whispered in a tremulous tone. "Are you very badly hurt?"

Stapleton shuddered and tried in vain to raise his right hand in order to touch Kinsella. His tortured face became radiant.

"Oh! Michael, I'm so glad," he muttered in a voice that was now almost unintelligible. "I was afraid you wouldn't be in time. Hold me. I don't want to fall down again. It mustn't be lying down. Don't let me fall."

Kinsella took him in his arms and whispered:

"Don't worry, George. I won't let you fall."

"There is still so much that I want to say," Stapleton muttered, "but there is no more time. The hour is nearly . . ."

He suddenly got an access of strength and clutched Kinsella firmly with both hands.

"Tell me about the flower again," he cried out in a voice that had regained its clarity and resonance. "It was so lovely and so generous, your black and scarlet flower, that showered its petals and then died, only to grow again at once, in eternal repetition of its . . ."

Madden turned aside as the dying man suddenly became silent. He licked his lower lip, frowned deeply and looked about the floor for the revolver that had been dropped. He found it a few feet away. He picked it up and thrust it into his pocket furtively, as if he were ashamed of what he was doing. Then he glanced at the door through which the singing men were leaving the room.

"He's gone," said Kinsella.

Madden took off his cap and crossed himself.

"Lord have mercy on his soul," he said solemnly.

He put on his cap again and watched Kinsella arrange Stapleton's body carefully in a sitting position against the wall. He kept shifting his feet restlessly and looking back over his shoulder at the departing men, nearly all of whom had now gone.

"Hurry, Captain," he cried out at length in a gruff voice.

"Just a moment," said Kinsella.

"Blood'n'ounds!" Madden said angrily. "What's the good of fiddling with him? The whole place is going to fall in a . . ."

"Silence," said Kinsella sternly as he got to his feet.

"Sorry, sir," Madden muttered, as he strode towards the door.

Now that his fallen comrade had passed beyond compassion, the hammer was beating time with extreme urgency inside his head, calling him to a renewal of dark rapture.

21

As soon as the insurgents began to issue from a northern side door of their headquarters into Henry Street, it became obvious that they had shot their bolt and that they would not go very far in their effort to break through encirclement, in spite of their fanatical enthusiasm. Only a small number of them, like Madden, were still vigorous enough to fight with any degree of efficiency. The others had apparently exhausted the little that remained of their strength by the defiant outburst of emotion in the assembly room and staggered helplessly as they walked across the street — like nervous horses that "run their race" during the parade in the paddock and can only flounder along in the ruck after the break from the starting gate.

Even so, it was a great tribute to their courage that they were still on their feet and eager to continue their heroic struggle, after being in action constantly for five days without relief of any sort, against an opponent that outnumbered them by fifty to one. Their opponent's superiority in weapons was greater still. Just now, the thunder of his artillery and the triumphant chatter of his machine guns offered a brutal contrast to their pathetic rifles and revolvers, most of which were secondhand and of obsolete design. Two of them had only shotguns, while another fellow's sole weapon was an eighteenth-century pike. They had very little ammunition left.

Fortunately, it was pitch dark at the point where they crossed the street, in a vacuum between two areas of brilliant firelight. So that they were able to pass without being detected into Henry Place, a narrow lane running northwards between Moore Street and Upper O'Connell Street. Otherwise, they would have been massacred then and there, owing to the slowness and disorder of their movement. Apart from their exhaustion, their straggling column was hampered by the presence of a great many noncombatants that required either assistance or surveillance. These included prisoners and a few women nurses and saffron-kilted boy scouts of a very tender age and a considerable number of severely wounded men who had to be carried on stretchers. Among the latter was James Connolly, the military commander of the whole insurgent force in Dublin. He had been crippled by a leg wound. Some members of the Provisional Government, that had been proclaimed on Monday, must also be included among the elements that hampered the movement of the column, owing to extreme old age or physical disability. No doubt the presence of these men inspired faith and confidence in their followers, who worshiped them for their qualities of mind and soul. During the cruel chess game of battle, however, all pieces that cannot be used effectively are a nuisance, since they interfere with the movement of the others across the board.

The lane ran north in a straight line for a short distance and then turned sharply west towards Moore Street. A few yards beyond the turn, another lane branched north from

221

it to Parnell Street, where a small group of imperial army soldiers were stationed behind a barricade. These soldiers were very efficient and alert, because they quickly detected the insurgent column that was moving westwards in furtive silence under cover of darkness and engaged the vanguard almost as soon as it had begun to pass the southern mouth of the lane. Their rifle fire had netted ten casualties before their startled opponent fully realized what was happening and came to a halt on both sides of the danger zone.

Kinsella and Madden were among those that had passed the mouth of the lane before the column came under fire. During the preparation for the sortie at headquarters, Kinsella had been given charge of fifteen men, with whose identity he was only vaguely familiar. Owing to the darkness and the confusion that followed a sudden halt under attack in a very confined space, the various units formed in such haphazard fashion at the last moment dissolved into a crowd that recognized no subdivision of authority. Thus Kinsella lost contact with most of his men. Only Madden and two others obeyed his order to throw themselves down and return the enemy fire. In any case, his voice was now so weak, owing to exhaustion and the shock of his friend's death, that it was audible only to those within a few feet of him. Another officer also brought some men into action at the far corner. In a few minutes, their combined fire had subdued the enemy sufficiently to allow the remainder of the column to pass westwards without very serious loss. All told, however, more than twenty men had been put out of action while crossing the mouth of the lane.

Kinsella was among those who got hit. It was only a

flesh wound in the left forearm and he continued to fire without paying any heed to it, until the last of the fallen had been removed and the men in action at the far corner had withdrawn. It was only after he had withdrawn his own men that he examined his arm and found that it was bleeding freely.

"Have you got any field dressing?" he asked Madden.

The Connemara man started violently. He himself had had a narrow escape while dropping prone to engage the enemy. A bullet struck the buckle of his belt and then glanced across his body through his fleece-lined coat, to find an exit just above his heart. In the joyous frenzy of being in action once more, he had remained unconscious of the incident until this moment. The trembling fear that the close brush with death now inspired in him, however, was not on his own account but on that of Kinsella. He was overwhelmed by the thought that his captain was seriously hurt. Indeed, during the past five days, fear that Kinsella might get killed was nearly always present at the back of his mind; although he had never consciously admitted the possibility of a catastrophe that would leave him once more without the wonderful security of having a leader to think for him and determine his conduct and justify his Idea.

"Where are you hit?" he cried in panic, as he fumbled at Kinsella in the darkness. "Is it bad?"

His voice had again become shrill and high-pitched.

"I'm all right, man," said Kinsella in an irritated tone. "It's only a scratch, but it's bleeding rather freely. Tie it up somehow."

Madden pulled out the packet of field dressing that Stapleton had not let him use.

223

"Thank God," he said in a tone of intense relief. "You put the heart crosswise in me, Captain. I was afraid . . ."

"Stop talking," Kinsella interrupted. "Look sharp. We must get back to our position at once."

"Take it easy, Captain," Madden said. "I'll have it done in a jiffy."

He slashed the sleeves of Kinsella's tunic and shirt with a jackknife that he had picked up while leaving the General Post Office. Then he opened the packet of field dressing and began to treat the wound with iodine.

"Never mind that," said Kinsella urgently. "Just bind it. We're in action again."

Now thoroughly informed of the insurgent movement, the imperial troops stationed in Parnell Street opened murderous fire with two machine guns, as the head of the column pushed beyond the corner of the lane into Moore Street. The insurgents turned back at once. Their leaders then conferred hurriedly and decided to charge up Moore Street with the most active of the men that remained on their feet, in an attempt to overwhelm the machine-gun nest at the far end. While hurried preparations were being made for this charge, the door of the house at the northern corner of the lane was broken down. The freshly wounded and those already on stretchers were brought into the house, together with the prisoners and the women and children.

The O'Rahilly, one of the principal insurgent leaders, led the charge. It was launched in such haste that Madden and Kinsella reached the head of the column only just in time to take part in it. As was only natural under such circumstances, it developed in utmost disorder. The men just plunged from the lane in a compact mass behind their

224

leader. They were met by a hail of bullets that knocked down about a fourth of their number before they had time to deploy across the narrow street. Indeed, most of those that remained standing made no attempt to deploy. Being without previous experience of such combat and not having been told what to do, they merely pressed together closely as they charged madly up the street towards the chattering machine guns, whose fire cut back and forth among them like a saw until they all lay prone. The few that had deployed continued to advance bravely until The O'Rahilly fell dead, halfway up the street. The survivors then broke and sought shelter.

Kinsella was running at the far side of the street, with Madden close at his heels, when he got hit. He fell right in front of the butcher's shop where Mrs. Colgan had taken refuge on the previous night.

Madden fell on top of him.

22

THE CONNEMARA MAN lay motionless for a few moments, stretched across his captain's back. His mind was without thought. His whole being was without feeling of any sort, as if he had been halted suddenly, by the violence of his passion, in a strange vacuum between life and death. Then fear smote him with great force at the pit of his stomach, rushed to his brain and set his hands in frenzied movement. Muttering unintelligible words, he groped at the body that lay under him.

As he touched the clothes along the back and shoulders, the unresisting flesh beneath increased his fear. Then he pawed at the head. It dangled helplessly on the axis of its neck, swaying from side to side in obedience to each thrust. Then like a foolish creature, he touched the lips and the eyes and the ears, frantically searching for a sign of life. In increasing panic, he hurriedly raised and dropped the arms, calling on them to show vigor. They were just as limp and unresisting as the head. Finally, he drew aside, turned the body over on its back and laid his ear close to the heart. He stopped chattering and listened intently for a little while. Hearing no sound come from within the ribs, he shuddered, raised his head a little and looked about him with his mouth open.

226

The machine guns had now stopped firing. The street was silent except for the low moaning of the wounded, who crawled like reptiles along the ground towards the far pavement, past the prone bodies of their comrades that lay motionless in death.

"He's gone," he said at length in a slow whisper.

He started on hearing this statement, as if it had been made by someone other than himself. A wild tumult broke out in his mind on receipt of the horrid news. There seemed to be hundreds of voices shouting there, although they made no sound. Each voice was lamenting a beauty that had just died. Dead! His captain was dead. Now the wings of the wild geese no longer whirred through the silent vastness of the starry firmament and the poet's voice was stilled. Order and the certainty of faith were both destroyed. He had again become a penniless vagabond, standing between two pillars of the portico, not knowing where to go or what to do, without a heroic purpose to glorify his life.

Dead! All that had raised him to the heights of ecstasy during the past five days was dead. All passion was spent.

Then he stiffened as the Idea came to life and silenced the lamenting voices with a fierce denial of defeat.

"It's a lie," he growled. "He's not dead."

Moving with great rapidity, he picked up his rifle and slung it across his back, thrust Kinsella's pistol into his coat pocket and drew the limp body into the doorway of the shop. Being then under cover, he jumped to his feet and hurled himself with all his force against the locked door. It was stoutly built and resisted his efforts for several minutes. Then it splintered at the center. He kicked

227

aside the broken boards, picked up the body in his arms and carried it through the hole into the shop.

At first there was total darkness in the room. Then a door at the far end creaked as it opened slightly. A narrow stream of light entered. A moment later, a man's face peered cautiously around the corner of the doorjamb. The face looked terrified.

"Who's that?" the man said in an awed whisper.

Without answering this question, Madden strode across the floor past the dressed carcasses of cattle and sheep that hung from iron hooks in the ceiling. He kicked the door open and entered a narrow hallway with his burden. Straight in front of him, a stairway led to the second floor. He took a pace towards the stairway, halted and then turned to the left along the hallway.

"You can't come in here," cried the man that had peered around the corner of the door. "There are women in the house."

He was Simon Tracy, the owner of the shop. He was powerfully built, with a bull neck, a bloated red face, small blue eyes and thinning red hair. He wore only an open waistcoat over his white shirt. His large belly overflowed the waistband of his blue serge trousers. He carried his left fist thrust out before his face and his right pressed close to his side, as he shuffled backwards before the advancing Connemara man, with the dancing movement of a boxer. In spite of his aggressive pose, his face still looked terrified. His mouth was wide open. He kept retreating hurriedly until he reached a small group of women that stood before the kitchen door, at the far end of the hallway.

Mrs. Colgan was among this group. She stepped forward

after Tracy had passed and peered at Madden intently, with her left hand shielding her eyes. She was still wearing her shawl, her white smock and her round black hat with the perpendicular white feather.

"Is that you, Bartly?" she said in a frightened tone.

Madden did not answer. His crazed eyes stared right over her head as he approached. He now moved with solemn slowness, like a man entranced, striking the floor heavily with the heels of his top boots. The rigidity of his carriage and the fierceness of his countenance contrasted sharply with the wanton shifting of his lifeless burden, whose hanging limbs dangled idly at each step; like sea plants that curl and stretch and get entwined, as they are bandied back and forth without resistance by the vast power of the swaying tide.

"Is that you, Bartly, in God's name?" Mrs. Colgan called out again.

As he passed without answering or showing any sign of recognition, she leaned forward and peered closely at Kinsella's face. Her tense features relaxed at once.

"Thanks be to God," she muttered, crossing herself.

Herding the other four members of the little group behind him, Tracy had now backed into the kitchen.

"You can't come in here," he protested once more, as Madden reached the door. "We don't want any trouble. None of us have anything to do with the rising. There are women here."

Madden had to stoop and turn sideways in order to go through the door with his burden.

"Thanks be to God and to His Blessed Mother," whispered Mrs. Colgan fervently, as she followed him into the kitchen. "You came back to me, my darling Bartly, just

229

as I knew you would and it's not my dead you are carrying in your arms."

The room was quite large, but it was so cluttered with furniture of various sorts that there was very little free space. It obviously served many purposes. Rather elegant parlor chairs, a sofa covered with black leather and a mahogany whatnot laden with family photographs stood against the walls, cheek by jowl with a large kitchen dresser and a sink that was crowded with dirty pots and dishes. A dining-room table, dressed in a fine linen cloth, stood in the center of the floor. A meal had just been consumed there. It was only partially cleared. The teapot, the butter, the sugar, the milk and a long flat dish containing several pieces of fried beefsteak remained on the board. There was a narrow bed in the corner farthest from the door. A thin old man was stretched on top of it, with his shoulders propped against two pillows, and his arms folded across his chest. He wore a threadbare black suit, carpet slippers and a bowler hat. He was smoking a clay pipe.

"This man is badly hurt," Madden cried out in a harsh voice, as he halted a short distance within the door. "Show me a proper place to lay him down."

Nobody answered him. Mrs. Colgan went on chattering in a low voice, with her hands clasped in front of her bosom and her birdlike face turned towards the ceiling. The old man puffed clouds of smoke from his pipe at regular intervals, as he watched the scene with solemn and detached interest. The butcher, his wife and three daughters continued to gape in terror at the Connemara man and his gruesome burden.

"Speak up," Madden continued, raising his voice to a

230

shout. "This man is a great captain and a hero. Tend to him quickly, or I'll take your lives. Where can I lay him down?"

Mrs. Colgan then stepped forward, touched Madden on the arm and pointed to the sofa.

"Put him down there, Bartly," she said.

Madden glanced at the black sofa and then started violently, as it evoked a somber memory in his crazed mind of a man stretched out in death and another lamenting.

"You devil's bitch!" he cried, as he turned on Mrs. Colgan. "It's not there I'll lay him down."

Then he strode across the floor to the bed and said to the old man:

"Get up out of there."

The old man calmly took another pull at his pipe and then swung his legs to the floor, staring at Madden in a detached manner. He got to his feet slowly and walked over to the range, still looking back over his shoulder at the Connemara man, without the least sign of emotion on his face. He brought a chair close to the grate and sat down with his feet together. There were little pink spots on the wrinkled yellow skin of his cheeks.

As Madden began to lay Kinsella's body on the bed with tender care, the butcher's wife came over to the old man on tiptoe. She was a short fat woman, with bulging blue eyes and tousled fair hair. The old man was her father.

"Don't be afraid, Dado," she whispered to him in a very nervous tone, as she put her hand on his thin shoulder. "He won't hurt you."

The old man stiffened, drew back his shoulders, took his pipe out of his mouth and spat into the grate. His sunken eyes were now aflame with anger. He rubbed his slippered feet backwards along the floor, one after the other, like a cock getting ready to fight. Then he glared at his daughter.

"Me afraid?" he cried in a shrill voice, as he tapped his chest with the stem of his pipe. "Is it me? Paddy Lenihan afraid? By the holy! What will I hear next?"

"Be quiet, Dado," whispered the butcher's wife.

"That be damned," the old man shouted. "I was never afraid of man or beast during the whole of my natural life and I'll fight anyone that dares to doubt my word."

Mrs. Colgan had now come up behind Madden and begun to whisper softly close to his ear, as he arranged the pillows under Kinsella's head. Her relief at finding that the dead body was not that of her son had passed and she was again tormented by unbearable anxiety. Yet Madden's strange attitude prevented her from asking him point-blank what had happened to Tommy. So that what she said was really only for the purpose of "getting inside his rage" and re-establishing friendly contact with the "miraculous protector."

"I tried to reach ye in the Post Office," she said, "but this was as far as I could get. It was, 'faith and only for the Blessed Virgin I wouldn't have got this far itself. Simon over there and Josephine, God bless the poor creatures, they kindly let me stay here, even though I'm hardly related to them at all, except through my husband, Lord have mercy on him, but sure it's only in time of woe that you get to know your own and a half stranger is often more loyal than a person of your deepest blood. It's true, 'faith. The other crowd let fly at me with their machine guns every time I showed my nose outside the house, trying to cross over towards the Post Office. Lord save us, Bartly,

232

the shower of bullets was so thick that even the smallest flea you ever saw in your life . . ."

She stopped chattering as Madden stood erect and made a peculiar sound in his throat. Then she stepped aside, leaned forward and looked up into his face. What she saw there made her start and draw back hurriedly, with horror in her eyes.

"Lord save us," she muttered, crossing herself. "What ails him now?"

Madden's nostrils kept expanding and contracting rapidly as he looked down at the corpse, with his head turned slightly sideways and his chin pressed hard against his throat; like a wild stallion of the western desert that stops dead in his tracks before his herd of mares and rises up with forelegs bent, taut like a compressed spring, to stamp upon a coiled rattlesnake.

"What made me do that?" he growled. "Why did I cross his hands on his chest and close his eyes?"

Then he whirled around and shouted:

"Tend to him quickly, or I'll kill the lot of you."

The butcher had now recovered from his terror and faced the Connemara man boldly, with the palms of his hands on his hips.

"What ails you at all, man?" he said in a quiet and placatory tone. "He is past tending now, the poor creature. Lord have mercy on him, he's as dead as a doornail."

Madden leaped forward with the rapidity of a great cat and clutched the butcher by the throat. Tracy's wife and daughters screamed as they saw him borne backwards to the far wall in one great rush.

"Fight him, Simon," shouted the old man. "Hit him in the belly with your knee."

233

The butcher grunted as he struck the wall. Then his fleshy body went limp and he opened his mouth wide, gasping for breath.

"You lying dog!" Madden growled. "He's not dead."

Even while he spoke, the chorus of lamenting voices broke out again in his mind, giving his own words the lie. He released the butcher's throat, turned about and drew the back of his right hand across his forehead. Then he staggered towards the table, with downcast head and drooping shoulders.

"You have him now, Simon," the old man cried in triumph, as he leaped up and down on his chair. "Keep after him."

The butcher's wife thumped the old man in the back and said:

"Shut your mouth, Dado."

Then she ran across to her husband, who had collapsed onto a chair.

"Sit down there, Bartly," Mrs. Colgan whispered in a motherly and ingratiating tone, as she helped Madden onto a chair by the table. "Sit down now, treasure, and cry your fill for your dead comrade, as is fitting for you. Cry for him, Bartly, and ask the Blessed Virgin to intercede for him before the throne of God."

In fact, Madden's shoulders convulsed and his lips fluttered and he made sounds of weeping in his throat. Yet his eyes remained tearless. Indeed, they looked fiercer than before as he stared at the board.

"Are you all right, Simon?" the butcher's wife said to her husband.

"I'm all right," said the butcher, rubbing his throat.

"Thank God for that," his wife said.

234

Then she ran to her three daughters, who stood close together by the dresser to the left of the door. They clutched one another and whimpered as they stared at Madden. Two of them were thirteen-year-old twins. The third was fifteen and almost fully grown, with well-developed breasts. All three of them were dressed in green and they had bits of pink ribbon tied to the ends of their plaited auburn hair.

"Go on upstairs out of that," their mother said to them.

She had to push them bodily out of the room.

"Go on up now," she cried, as she drove them along the hallway. "The shooting has stopped outside, so you needn't be afraid. Go on up to the room and stop whining, like good girls."

Mrs. Colgan went over to the bed and peered at the corpse.

"It's Tommy's boss all right," she said to herself.

Then her anxiety became so acute that she could bear it no longer and she rushed back to Madden.

"Is it how you have him hidden somewhere, Bartly?" she whispered, as she leaned over his shoulder. "Tell me, treasure. Did you leave him in a safe place?"

Madden went on staring at the table, without showing any sign of having heard what she said.

" 'Faith, you did right to hide him," she continued, "same as a she goat hides her kid, when she's too busy to mind it. Arrah! How could you look after my little one while you had the boss in your arms and the other crowd blasting at you? You had to hide him, 'faith. Indeed, you had. Ah! My little treasure! He must be hardly able to walk at all, after being out there for five long days and nights, without rest or sleep. What else could you do but leave him behind? Whisper to me, Bartly. Is the place you hid him far from here?"

Madden raised his head and looked at her with recognition. His physical crisis had now passed. The voices had ceased their tumult and his mind was clear. Except for the deadly look in his eyes, his face was perfectly composed.

"Is that you, good woman?" he said gruffly.

"Indeed it is, Bartly," she said. "Praised be God, you are yourself again. What news have you got for me, treasure?"

He licked his lips, swallowed his spittle with a wry grimace and said harshly:

"Give me a drink."

"I will and welcome, darling," she said. "I'll give you a cup of tea out of this pot."

She brought a fresh cup from the dresser and filled it from the teapot on the table.

"It's half cold now," she said, as she added milk and sugar, "but it's better for the thirst that way."

The butcher's wife came into the room at that moment.

"I'll wet a fresh cup for him," she cried out in a high-pitched voice, as she hurried to the table. "There is a good bit of the meat left, too. Hand him a plate of it. If it's not enough, I can throw a couple of eggs and a bit of bacon on the pan."

The old man stamped on the floor with both feet and shouted:

"Are ye crazy, women? Are ye feeding a man that might rise up and kill us all when his belly is full?"

"Shut up, Dado," said Mrs. Tracy.

236

Madden took the cup from Mrs. Colgan and drank all the tea at once. Then he looked at her in silence for a few moments.

"I'd be putting a sin on my immortal soul," he said at length in a solemn tone, "if I told you anything but the truth."

She was standing close behind him while he spoke. After he had finished, she stepped back hurriedly and crossed herself. Her little face had lost all its color and her eyes narrowed to slits.

"Speak up, then," she said. "I'm not afraid to hear whatever God has ordained for me to hear."

Madden again looked at her in silence for a few moments.

"Speak up," she repeated. "Is he dead?"

"I don't know, good woman," Madden said in a low voice. "I don't know whether he's dead or alive. Two days ago, he ran out of a place where there was fighting and I didn't see him since. I didn't hear tale or tidings of him, either. So I couldn't tell you what has happened to him. He may be still alive, but then again he may be dead. He might have been with the crowd of us that left the General Post Office a short while ago and on the other hand he mightn't. That's all I can tell you."

Mrs. Tracy came over from the range and put her arms around Mrs. Colgan.

"You poor creature!" she whimpered. "Oh! You poor little creature!"

Mrs. Colgan thrust the butcher's wife aside and then faced Madden belligerently, with her little hands on her hips. She was really intensely relieved by what Madden had told her, because she had feared the worst from the

237

moment she saw him come along the hallway in a demented state; even though what he was then carrying proved not to be her son. Through her limitless and unreasoning faith, she was now convinced by what he had said that Tommy was still alive and safe under the protection of the Blessed Virgin. If he did run away from "a place where there was fighting," it was obvious to her that his act was inspired by the Mother of God. Even so, she now hated Madden bitterly for having suggested that her beloved son was a coward.

"Is that all you have to tell me?" she whispered fiercely.

"Take it easy, good woman," Madden said to her in the same solemn tone. "It's better to leave the rest unsaid, because at this hour I can only speak the truth. So take it easy, I'm telling you."

"So he ran away according to you," she whispered.

"He did that and more," Madden said, "but what he did is not worth talking about, in a room where a hero lies dead."

Then she shook herself from head to foot, and shouted:

"Ho! Listen to the man that talks of heroes and casts aspersions on a widow's only son. Listen to that spalpeen that I found, dirty and hungry, without a penny in his pocket, that I brought home and fed and cleaned and put to bed, that I had to drag through the streets with me and he so terrified that he tried to hide behind his back the gun that I had put into his fist. Listen to him, good people. Listen to the barefaced liar that promised to bring me back my little one and then comes and calls that little one a coward. Look at the fine coat that's on the dirty robber's back and the elegant top boots on his legs, this penniless

238

spalpeen that I found wandering about the streets and brought home with me, through the goodness of my heart."

The old man jumped to his feet and approached the table with his little hands clenched.

"Give it to him, Mary Anne," he shouted in his piping voice. "Give it to the cowardly bully."

The butcher also got to his feet and approached Madden, eager to have revenge for the recent insult to his manhood. All four of them now stood around the Connemara man in a hostile attitude, like mongrel dogs about a wolf-hound which they suspect of having become inoffensive.

"Look at the shameless one," Mrs. Colgan continued in a shrill and venomous tone. "Look at the highway robber that says my son ran out of a place where there was fighting. Is it my son? Is it the son of Mary Anne Joyce? Is it a Madden that's casting the word 'coward' into the face of a Joyce from Maam Valley?"

As she drew back a little and pointed at him with her outstretched right hand, Madden sat erect and looked at her darkly.

"Be silent, woman," he said in a very solemn tone. "You are in the presence of my dead."

"The devil a bit of me," she retorted. "I'm going to tell you what I think of the Maddens before I stop. Ye are a scum of tinkers and sheep stealers and informers, that should be driven out of the West by bell, book and candle-light."

Madden jumped to his feet with startling suddenness and drew his American pistol from its holster.

"Get out of here," he cried as he rose, "and leave me alone with my dead. Get out."

All four of them drew back hastily a little way and then stood gaping at him.

"Get out," he cried again. "Ye are an insult to a hero that died for ye. Clear out of here, before I put murder on my soul in the house of my dead."

They fled pell-mell from the room, urging one another to make haste. He followed them to the door.

"Don't come back here, any of you," he called after them, as they ran along the hallway. "I'll shoot anybody that tries to come in here."

He closed the door, put his back to it and stared at the far wall.

"I'll stay with him until morning," he said aloud.

He stood that way for a long time, staring at the wall, with his pistol in his hand. Now and again, he licked his lower lip and made a wry grimace. Then he started, put his pistol in its holster, walked very erect and stiff-legged to the bed, took off his cap, crossed his arms on his chest and looked down at the corpse.

He shuddered as he saw the matted blood on the torn breast of the tunic. For a few moments, his sorrow for his dead captain became "human" and soft. Then he raised his glance to the face and his sorrow hardened. The face had not been touched by the bullets. It was just as strong in death as it had been in life. Even without the eyes, that were now closed forever, the finely chiseled features still bore witness to the gentle lordliness and discipline of the intellect that had ruled them.

As he looked at this face, which had saved him from the trembling indecision of a slave that shrank from bearing arms for the Idea of freedom, the hammer began to strike once more in slow and steady rhythm inside his head.

23

ᒣᒣᒣᒣᒣᒣᒣᒣᒣᒣᒣᒣᒣᒣᒣᒣᒣᒣᒣ

HE STOOD GUARD over his dead captain until break of day. Then he cleaned and reloaded all his weapons, ate most of the meat that remained in the dish, took a last look at the corpse, put on his cap and left the room. A gas lamp still burned in the hallway. There was no sound of life in the house. The others had taken the girls and fled by a back way, immediately after being expelled from the kitchen.

He halted on reaching the broken door of the shop and listened intently for a few moments. All was still in the street outside. There was no sound of firing anywhere in the city. He drew two pistols and stepped through the hole. Then he halted abruptly, on seeing the door of the house directly opposite being opened slightly. A short piece of stick, to which a white cloth was attached, was thrust through the opening and waved several times, back and forth.

"Blood'n'ounds!" he growled, as he stared at the white cloth that was tied to the top of the stick. "What does that mean?"

The insurgents had worked far into the night, boring a passage northwards through the houses on the far side of the street. Overcome by exhaustion, they abandoned this

241

last attempt at coming to close quarters with their enemies, on reaching the house from which the white flag of truce was now being waved.

"Blood'n'ounds!" Madden growled again, as he saw a young woman emerge from the house with a flag. "That crowd must be going to quit."

The young woman was in insurgent uniform. She was bareheaded and her coiled hair was in disorder. She looked about her nervously on reaching the pavement. Then she headed north at a slow uncertain pace, towards the barricade behind which the imperial soldiers stood in wait. A few of those fallen in the charge were still stretched on the roadway. She shied away from the corpses, like a frightened filly, with her eyes and her nostrils distended.

There was no sign of the inhabitants until she had advanced about fifteen yards. Then heads began to appear at the doors and windows of the brick-faced two-storied houses on both sides of the street; like the heads of rabbits peeping from the multiple holes of their warren, to see if an intruder has departed. At first they stared at her in silence, unable to appreciate the import of her journey and of the white flag she carried. Then they began to whisper timidly to one another from house to house, asking what was afoot. Finally, they took courage and addressed the young woman herself in less subdued tones.

She paid no heed to their questions. Holding the stick before her upraised face with both hands, like a person carrying a cross in a religious procession, she marched on in silence until she reached the barricade. There she spoke for a little while to the officer in charge of the soldiers. Then she turned and marched back again at a much faster pace. Her head was now downcast and her shoulders

242

drooped. She carried the white flag limply by her side.

The people now called out boldly to her as she passed.

"God love you, darling," one woman said. "Is the fight over? Are ye going to quit at last?"

"It's about time, too," another woman cried angrily. "Ye have been torturing us poor people long enough."

An old man shook his fist at her from a doorway and shouted:

"You shameless creature! What do you mean by going about the streets without a hat or a shawl to cover your head?"

The young woman kept quickening her pace as she marched in silence down the long narrow corridor, from both sides of which an ever-growing chorus of voices assailed her. Most of the voices were hostile. Even the few sympathetic ones gave her no support in her distasteful task, being querulous and forlorn, like birds that hail a snowy dawn of hunger and cold. Unable to bear the strain any longer, she burst into tears as she approached the house from which she had emerged.

"Blood'n'ounds!" Madden growled as he watched her re-enter the house in tears. "That crowd is going to surrender all right."

He drew a little farther back into the doorway and put away his pistols. He had come out of the house with the intention of rejoining "that crowd," in order to continue the fight with them. Now that they were going to surrender, however, he no longer felt associated with them in any way. His last link with them had been broken. He was completely alone with his Idea.

"I had better be on my way," he said.

Yet he did not move. His unique passion had now en-

243

tered its last phase and had no purpose other than that of being. Even the power and beauty of his captain's dead face had been absorbed in the composition of his dark rapture. So that he felt perfectly fulfilled, standing there alone before the broken door, ready to defend the dignity of a free man in arms against all comers.

The door opposite had been closed behind the young woman. Now it was thrown wide open and two imperial soldiers, who had been made prisoner by the insurgents, came out of the house. They carried a stretcher, on which a third soldier lay under a blanket. As they were turning north along the pavement, a young woman in nurse's uniform came out of the house with another blanket. The two soldiers halted the stretcher to let her wrap the blanket about their wounded comrade.

Patrick Pearse came out of the house as the stretcher was on the point of moving forward once more. On catching sight of the poet, the wounded man raised his head, uttered a cry and stretched out his arms. The poet smiled and bent over him. The wounded man then put his arms around Pearse's neck and the two men embraced. After they had disengaged, the poet shook the man's hand and then marched up the street towards the barricade, followed by the stretcher.

The people leaning from the doors and windows had been chattering in vulgar excitement since the passage of the young woman with the flag. They watched the poet's march in silence. Some obscure element of godliness, that lay dormant in their souls, made them bow down in silent reverence before this lordly man; as if they understood that he was walking to his death, in order to give them the dignity of freedom. Even after he had been taken out of sight, by the officer in charge of the barricade, they held their tongues. When he reappeared some time later and came walking back without his sword, many of them crossed themselves and asked him for his blessing.

Madden had watched this whole scene without thought or feeling of any sort.

"I had better be going now," he whispered, after Pearse had gone back into the house. "I must be on my way."

Again he paid no heed to this suggestion, being held to the spot on which he stood by some force that was beyond the power of his will. Now, however, his mind was no longer empty. Images of stark beauty, from his native earth and sea, passed in solemn procession across the horizon of his memory. His feet began to itch and the hammer increased the rate of its striking against his forehead.

The inhabitants of the street had broken out into a frenzied chatter of argument after the poet's return to the house. They became silent once more, on seeing him re-emerge. He was now accompanied by all the other surviving leaders. James Connolly was carried on a stretcher and Joseph Plunkett was so weak that he had to be assisted in his walk. As the group advanced, many people came out onto the pavements and knelt in prayer. A few of them even ran into the roadway, touched the clothes of those walking to their death and then crossed themselves.

When the leaders had passed behind the barricade, the main body of the insurgents came out of the houses they had occupied and laid down their arms in the street.

"Now is the time," Madden cried aloud, as he drew his pistols.

24

WATCHING on the far side of the street with the butcher's family, Mrs. Colgan saw her son come out of the house that bordered on the lane. Uttering wild cries of joy, she ran over and clasped him in her arms.

"Oh! My little darling!" she cried, with tears rolling down her cheeks, as she hugged and kissed him. "She sent you back to me, alive and well. Thanks be to the Mother of God. She sent you back to me. My treasure! Oh! My own little treasure!"

She had to be forcibly separated from him as the men formed into a column for their northward march. Then she got down on her knees in the roadway, raised her clasped hands above her head and gave fervent thanks to the Blessed Virgin. When the column moved forward, she got to her feet and trotted along its flank beside her son.

"Have no fear, Tommy," she whispered, as she leaned towards him. "I know they won't hurt you. It's only the big fish that get eaten. The little ones are thrown back alive into the sea. While you're in prison, be obedient to whoever is put over you. Then you'll soon be let out again. Now that the fight is over, put all hatred out of your heart. That'll make it easy for you to be biddable. It will, 'faith. When they see you have forgiven, they'll forget. You'll soon be back with me again. God's Blessed Mother has brought you this far and she'll bring you the rest of the way, too, safe and sound. Say your prayers, morning, noon and night. Shun bad company and guard your faith in God. Then you'll be all right, little one."

Madden looked at her and Tommy without recognition, as they passed the doorway in which he stood. With hard strained eyes he watched the disarmed insurgents tramp past him into captivity, without any feeling for them. When they had all gone, he crossed himself with the muzzle of his American pistol and stepped out onto the pavement.

"In God's name," he muttered, as he turned to the right.

He turned right again almost at once and marched westwards into the lane that led to the little square. He walked very slowly and stiff-legged. After he had gone a few yards, three soldiers hailed him from the far end of the lane. They called on him to halt and drop his guns and raise his hands above his head. He stared at them in wild delight and continued to advance at a leisurely pace, still carrying his pistols idly by his sides. They pointed their weapons and shouted at him again, saying they would fire if he did not halt. When he saw their bodies stiffen for the kill, he leveled his pistols, raised a shout and charged, firing as he came at them. One of his bullets found its mark and a soldier fell. The other two returned his fire. His attack had been launched with such suddenness and he came upon them with such great speed, dodging from side to side, that their first shots missed him, so that he felled another soldier before he himself was touched. Then a bullet from the third man's rifle pierced his stomach, when he was only a few yards from the square. He swerved and then was carried forward again

247

by his momentum. He discharged his Mauser into the skull of the man that had wounded him, as he went hurtling past into the square. Then he fell.

As he was getting to his feet again, several other soldiers opened fire. Three more bullets struck him. He discharged his pistols twice without effect and then dropped to the ground a second time. As he tried to rise again, he found that he could not use his legs. So he continued to fire from the ground until a bullet pierced his head. Then the soldiers approached.

All round the little square, people stared in silence from doors and windows at the dead body that lay prone, with a rifle slung across its back and each outstretched hand gripping a pistol.

Date Due